Praise for T. A. Barron's Merlin saga:

"An extraordinary journey of mind, body, and spirit—both for Merlin and for ourselves."   —Madeleine L'Engle

"Rich with magic."   —*The New York Times Book Review*

"In this brilliant epic, T. A. Barron has created a major addition to that body of literature, ancient and modern, dealing with the towering figure of Merlin. Barron combines the wellsprings of mythical imagination with his own deepest artistic powers. Through the ordeals, terrors, and struggles of Merlin-to-be, we follow an intense and profoundly spiritual adventure."
          —Lloyd Alexander

"This is a brilliant epic tale with memorable and glowing characters—a real gift."   —Isabel Allende,
          author of *House of the Spirits* and *Daughter of Fortune*

"All the elements of a classic here."
          —Robert Redford, actor, director, and conservationist

"Barron has created not only a magical land populated by remarkable beings but also a completely magical tale . . . that will enchant readers."
          —*Booklist* (boxed review), on *The Lost Years of Merlin*

"Set on the legendary island of Fincayra, this novel about the childhood of the wizard Merlin is imaginative and convincing."
          —*The Horn Book*, on *The Lost Years of Merlin*

"The quest for one's true identity, of puzzles and tests of intelligence, and moral courage are all here. . . . The climactic ending offers a twist to seeking one's identity and heritage. A good bet for those who enjoy fantasy, mythical quests, and of course, Merlin, the greatest wizard of them all."
          —*VOYA*, on *The Lost Years of Merlin*

"Barron never falters in creating a believable past for the greatest enchanter of all time."

—*Family Life* (Critic's Choice review),
on *The Lost Years of Merlin*

"With each book, Barron's *Lost Years of Merlin* saga just keeps getting richer in characterization, ambience, and Celtic lore. . . . Fans will definitely be clamoring for more."

— *Booklist*, on *The Fires of Merlin*

"For those who love the Merlin and Great Tree of Avalon series, Basil will be a welcome new friend."

—*VOYA*, on *Merlin's Dragon*

"No one can compare to Barron when writing about Merlin or Avalon. Once again, he brings texture, color, and love to the seven realms. His many fans will gobble up this new offering."

—*School Library Journal*,
on *Merlin's Dragon: Doomraga's Revenge*

"The many fans of Barron's various Merlin sagas will not be disappointed." —*Booklist*, on *Merlin's Dragon: Ultimate Magic*

★ "Liberally laced with humor and wit . . . readers will relish this fine . . . fantasy series." —*Booklist*, starred review,
on *The Great Tree of Avalon: Child of the Dark Prophecy*

"Barron crafts vivid scenes with original and well-developed supporting characters, moving the plot at a gobble-it-up pace."

—*KLIATT*,
on *The Great Tree of Avalon: Shadows on the Stars*

"Barron's world is fully realized and sophisticated, and fans of high fantasy will undoubtedly enjoy . . . this well-written, suspenseful story." —*VOYA*,
on *The Great Tree of Avalon: The Eternal Flame*

Do not underestimate Basil!

The colliding dragons shrieked, while bones cracked and scales splintered. When all the clouds of ash finally cleared, Lo Valdearg lay sprawled upon the body of his leader. Moaning in pain, he rolled off and slammed to the ground. The orange dragon, whose back had been broken, never moved again.

Confused, distraught, and thoroughly frightened, the other dragons scattered in all directions. They leaped into the air and flew away as fast as they could, not daring to look back, lest the bold green dragon decide to pursue them.

At the scene of the battle, Basilgarrad surveyed the remains of the attackers. Just beyond the crushed corpse, Lo Valdearg, unable to fly, crawled away in anguish. After watching him for a few seconds, Basilgarrad delivered the most humiliating blow of all: He simply turned away.

Swinging around to face Merlin—who, along with Hallia and Krystallus, gazed at him with grateful admiration—the green dragon narrowed his eyes. With gusto, he declared, "Let that be a warning to anybody who dares to call me a pet."

READ THE WHOLE MERLIN SAGA!

MERLIN

BOOK 7

DOOMRAGA'S REVENGE

T. A. BARRON

PUFFIN BOOKS
An Imprint of Penguin Group (USA) Inc.

PUFFIN BOOKS
Published by the Penguin Group
Penguin Young Readers Group, 345 Hudson Street, New York, New York 10014, U.S.A.
Penguin Group (Canada), 90 Eglinton Avenue East, Suite 700, Toronto, Ontario, Canada M4P 2Y3
(a division of Pearson Penguin Canada Inc.)
Penguin Books Ltd, 80 Strand, London WC2R 0RL, England
Penguin Ireland, 25 St Stephen's Green, Dublin 2, Ireland (a division of Penguin Books Ltd)
Penguin Group (Australia), 250 Camberwell Road, Camberwell, Victoria 3124, Australia
(a division of Pearson Australia Group Pty Ltd)
Penguin Books India Pvt Ltd, 11 Community Centre,
Panchsheel Park, New Delhi - 110 017, India
Penguin Group (NZ), 67 Apollo Drive, Rosedale, Auckland 0632, New Zealand
(a division of Pearson New Zealand Ltd.)
Penguin Books (South Africa) (Pty) Ltd, 24 Sturdee Avenue,
Rosebank, Johannesburg 2196, South Africa

Registered Offices: Penguin Books Ltd, 80 Strand, London WC2R 0RL, England

First published in the United States of America as *Merlin's Dragon: Doomraga's Revenge* by
Philomel Books, a division of Penguin Young Readers Group, 2009
Published as *Doomraga's Revenge* by Puffin Books,
a division of Penguin Young Readers Group, 2011

5 7 9 10 8 6 4

Patricia Lee Gauch, Editor

Text copyright © Thomas A. Barron, 2009
Map of Fincayra copyright © Ian Schoenherr, 1996
Map of Avalon copyright © Thomas A. Barron, 2003
All rights reserved

THE LIBRARY OF CONGRESS HAS CATALOGED THE PHILOMEL BOOKS EDITION AS FOLLOWS:
Barron, T. A. Merlin's dragon. Book two: Doomraga's revenge / by T. A. Barron.
p. cm.
Summary: The dragon Basil, now grown mighty in strength, size, and courage, addresses
and seeks the cause of a new series of crises that threaten the stability of Avalon,
while his friend Merlin is distracted by problems with his son, Krystallus.
ISBN: 978-0-399-25212-9 (hc)
[1. Dragons—Fiction. 2. Magic—Fiction. 3. Fathers and sons—Fiction. 4. Fantasy.]
I. Title
II. Title: Doomraga's revenge.
PZ7.B27567 Mer 2009 [Fic]—dc22 2008055872

Puffin Books ISBN 978-0-14-241925-0

Design by Semadar Megged
Text set in ITC Galliard

Printed in the United States of America

JUN 2016

Dedicated to the five little dragons
with big spirits
who shared our home

CONTENTS

1: NOT SO SMALL ANYMORE

Having been very small, I can truthfully tell you that size doesn't matter at all.

Except when it does.

The wrathful roar exploded—so forcefully it toppled a grove of ironwood trees, emptied a flowing river, and blew an entire waterfall sideways. Fierce winds slammed into the pinnacles high above Lavadon Lake, breaking off towers of rock that plunged over the cliffs encircling the lake, hitting the water with tumultuous splashes. Not that those splashes could be heard, however. The roar filled the air, overwhelming every other sound.

When, at last, the roar faded away, another sound remained. Higher and thinner it was, yet every bit as arresting—a frenzied chorus of shrieks.

The shrieks of children about to die.

Atop those sheer cliffs huddled a band of young dwarves. Like all their kind in Fireroot, curly red hair hovered over their heads like fluffy clouds. Yet their typical expressions of mischief and playfulness had given way to something else. Terror.

No adult dwarves stood by to protect them. All those who had tried, their mothers with sharp eyes and powerful hands and their fathers with brawny arms and thick beards, now lay in the dirt, their lifeless bodies smashed or shredded or incinerated. Not far away, glaring at the children, was the monster who had done this: Fireroot's most ferocious dragon.

"Tell me!" he commanded, scraping the ground with his murderous claws, slicing boulders as easily as a knife would cut a melon.

Lo Valdearg was the name he had chosen, hoping to link himself to Valdearg, the most dangerous dragon of ancient lore who had terrorized Merlin's isle of Fincayra. Although he'd only recently started causing havoc in Fireroot, the mere sound of this dragon's name, like his roar, made people quake in fear. As did the sight of his gigantic form, which was impossibly large, covered with scarlet scales that shielded his head, neck, chest, tail, and wings.

"Tell me!" he repeated, lifting his gargantuan head high above the cowering dwarves. To them, his massive face loomed as huge as a hillside. But this hillside had fiery red eyes and a vast mouth with rows of pinnacle-sharp teeth. Not to mention the ability to breathe fire hot enough to melt any stone.

Steaming hot air blew down on them from his cavernous nostrils, making the children shriek louder and forcing them to move back to the very edge of the cliff. They stood there, some of them holding hands and others covering their eyes, while the youngest children sat on the ground and wailed. Meanwhile, Lo Valdearg's ragged black beard, sprouting from the tip of his chin, slapped the air as he shook his massive head. From the beard fell drops of fresh blood, as well as a few remains of his latest victims—a severed arm here, an empty boot there.

"Tell me!" he demanded again, his voice rising to a roar.

"Never," cried an older girl, still clutching her father's charred ax. She raised the heavy ax as high as she could before her arms couldn't hold it any longer. As the double-edged blade slammed back to the ground, she spat, "We'll never tell you where to find the flaming jewels."

"Our people discovered them!" yelled a boy at her side.

"They belong to dwarves," called another. "Not dragons!"

Lo Valdearg's eyes glowed like molten lava. A ferocious rumble gathered in his chest, while his eyes seemed to burst into flames. "They will soon belong to me, you stubborn little insects."

The scarlet dragon drew a deep breath, preparing to blast his prey into ashes.

The shrieks rose louder, piercing the air. Many children shrank back, nearly falling over the edge. Only a few, including the girl with the ax, stood motionless before their foe.

He roared. Out of his mouth poured an avalanche of flames, so intensely hot that even the air itself seemed to flee, rushing away in a superheated wind. All this fire, smoke, and wind shot toward the young dwarves—

But never reached them.

At the instant the dragon's flames blasted forth, a great wing reached down from the sky and blocked the onslaught.

Protected by thousands of bright green scales, the wing deflected everything right back at the attacker, smothering him with smoke and fire.

Lo Valdearg roared—this time not with rage, but with surprise and pain. The sudden blast of flames had singed his eyes and burned away most of his beard. He rolled backward, away from the cliff, clawing at his wounded eyes.

At the same time, the creature whose wing had saved the children landed between them and Lo Valdearg. Smashing down with a resounding crash, his weight shook the ground violently—so violently that hundreds of boulders broke off from the cliff and rained down on the lake far below.

Gazing up at their savior, the children seemed frozen, too startled to speak. Partly because he was so huge—even bigger than their attacker, more like a mountain than anything alive. And partly because he was, to their utter astonishment, another dragon.

The great green dragon turned his head toward the children, still keeping one eye on the writhing body of Lo Valdearg. Lit by the stars of Avalon above, the scales on his brow sparkled like emeralds. "Do not fear me," he declared, his voice as loud as thunder yet somehow not so frightening. "I am Basilgarrad."

Still none of the children spoke. Their faces full of awe and disbelief, they merely continued to gawk at this enormous being who had appeared so suddenly. Some of the youngest dwarves continued to sob, while others started to crawl away from the edge of the cliff. At last, the girl with the ax thumped its blade on the ground. Peering up into one of the enormous green eyes, she shouted to be heard.

"Are you *the* Basilgarrad? Who saved Merlin from an evil kreelix?"

The titanic head nodded ever so slightly. But the dragon's eyes narrowed as he remembered his battle with the kreelix— whose power to devour magic often meant death for wizards . . . as well as dragons.

The girl glanced down at her ax. The sudden recollection of her father, who had wielded it so bravely until the moment of his death, filled her eyes with mist. Lifting her face again to Basilgarrad, she asked, "Why did you help us?"

Turning from the other dragon, who had rolled even farther away and was still clawing at his eyes in agony, Basilgarrad lowered his head a bit more. As his immense shadow covered the girl, many other dwarves backed away nervously. But she stood motionless, staring up at him.

Finally, the green dragon spoke, his voice surprisingly gentle. "Because, little one, I was once very small. Even smaller than you."

She blinked, unable to comprehend such a thing, let alone believe it. How could a creature with wings that could stretch across a valley ever have been small?

Sensing her doubt, Basilgarrad chuckled, a rich, bubbling sound that echoed deep in his throat. As his enormous lips parted, they revealed teeth sharper than spears, arrayed in rows, packed together like thousands of sentries. Except for one place, at the front of his mouth, where a prominently placed tooth was missing—the result of his battle with the kreelix.

A sudden roar burst upon them, flattening the girl and the rest of the dwarves with its force. Basilgarrad whirled around just as the scarlet dragon leaped at him, wings spread wide and deadly claws extended. Fire still glowed amidst the embers of the singed beard. Yet the attacker's angry eyes, swollen from burns, glowed even brighter.

"How dare you challenge me?" roared Lo Valdearg, spitting flames as he charged. "How dare you defy the greatest dragon of all time?"

With a single deft movement, Basilgarrad spun to the side. Whipping his enormous tail skyward, he slammed it into the attacker's belly, with such force that Lo Valdearg bellowed in pain and flipped upside down in the air. Then, before the dragon could recover, Basilgarrad swung his tail again, wrapping its length around his foe's neck. With a mighty roar of his own, so loud it was heard leagues away in the Volcano Lands, Basilgarrad hurled the scarlet dragon over the cliff and down into the lake below. A huge splash erupted, reaching even the highest rim of rock, spraying the young dwarves with water.

Silence slowly returned, broken only by the fading echoes of dragon roars and the slap of waves against the shore far below. Basilgarrad turned again to the girl with the ax. Her cheeks glistened with water from the splash, as a lone drop rolled down her nose. Though she was smaller than the smallest scale on his body, she gazed up at him without fear. Her upturned face glowed with gratitude.

"Thank you," she said. Basilgarrad gave a nod, while folding his immense wings against his back. She watched him for a moment, then added, "But I really can't believe you were ever small."

"Oh, but I was," he rumbled. His great green eye gave her a wink. "It does come in handy, though, that I'm not so small anymore."

2: WHISPERS

Revenge, for a dragon, is sometimes sweet, sometimes sour—but always tasty.

Fireroot was not Basilgarrad's favorite realm. *Too much sulfur in the air, too few trees on the ground,* as he'd once told Merlin.

Nevertheless, Basilgarrad stayed there long enough to help the young dwarves rejoin their people, guiding them to a tunnel entrance a few leagues away. Elder dwarves emerged and took the orphans into their homes; a few even thanked the dragon for his service. But when he offered to help dispose of the bodies of Lo Valdearg's victims, they refused, stubbornly insisting that only dwarves could do the grim work of a traditional burial.

Last of everyone to leave was the brave girl who carried her father's scorched ax. As she thanked him, she revealed that she'd been named after her grandmother Urnalda—a powerful leader of the dwarves long ago, in the days of Merlin's youth. Meanwhile, her eyes shone with a glint that assured him they would meet again. Then she raised the ax in a salute and followed the others into the tunnel.

Flying home over the blackened lands of this realm, he gazed down at a row of lava-spewing volcanoes. Sulfurous fumes clogged the air, making him crinkle his snout. Those charred summits and smoking ridges, ringed with noxious clouds of ash, seemed a fitting home for a murderer such as Lo Valdearg. But why had the scarlet dragon started that rampage? Why had his long-smoldering greed for the dwarves' precious jewels suddenly burst into deadly flames?

Banking sideways to avoid a towering cloud of ash, Basilgarrad grimaced. Not just because of the rancid smell, but because of something else on his mind. Lo Valdearg was, indeed, a problem—but not the only problem. More and more, outbreaks of violence were appearing around Avalon: raging dragons in Fireroot, thieving gnomes in Mudroot, tree-strangling snakes in northern Woodroot. Merlin, for his part, had been spending much more time recently dealing with such problems, doing his best to restore peace—and asking his friend to do the same. Still, the wizard didn't seem too troubled by the outbreaks, merely shrugging his shoulders and calling them "the growing pains of a young world." The great green dragon wasn't so sure.

He beat his wings more slowly, gliding above the dark, fire-blasted hills. His thoughts, meanwhile, traveled far away, across the seven realms of Avalon. His world. For all its bizarre and sometimes dangerous inhabitants, Avalon thrived on its wondrous diversity—and from the beginning had seemed the true home of peace and harmony.

Until now, that is. Why am I feeling so uneasy?

His huge wings beat the air, sending reverberations across the ashen hills. "You worry too much," he grumbled aloud. "If Merlin isn't concerned, why should you be? Time to stop—"

A piercing shriek cut him off. His green eyes opened wide, and he veered sharply to the left, pumping his enormous wings to fly straight toward the source of the terrifying sound. For he knew that sound all too well.

He plunged into a cloud whose fetid odors stung his eyes and assaulted his nose. But he kept flying straight ahead. That shriek meant that every second mattered. Again it came, this time joined by several more shrieks—equally cacophonous, equally terrifying.

Bursting out of the fetid cloud, he saw them: a gang of deadly dactylbirds. Scraping the air with their dagger-sharp talons, they flapped their large, leathery wings in unison. Nearing their prey—a flock of tiny, blue-winged mist faeries—they shrieked boisterously, as if they were already celebrating their kill.

Their wings slapped at the air, while their heavy-lidded eyes gleamed in triumph. Just ahead, the mist faeries flew in a frenzied panic, trying desperately to escape. Their delicate blue wings, each as thin as a wisp of mist, already showed tattered edges. Soon they would shred completely, leaving the faeries at the mercy of these predators.

The dactylbirds' shrieks grew louder, ripping at the air as violently as their talons often ripped at flesh. Then, without warning, their shrieking ceased.

An enormous green wing suddenly swept through the air. Catching all the killer birds by surprise, the wing folded over them and hurled them down—straight into the mouth of a fiery volcano. They had no time to resist or change course. Their raucous shrieks returned, though only briefly, before the volcano's bubbling hot lava swallowed them whole.

Basilgarrad stretched his wing again, soaring on high. As he watched the dactylbirds disappear, he recalled his own terror when others of their kind had pursued him in his younger, smaller days. He gazed for a while at the fuming volcano, then nodded with satisfaction. A new gleam in his eye, he muttered dryly, "That'll warm their hearts."

A cloud of blue mist blurred his vision. The faeries! They swarmed all around his face, wings whirring, calling to him in their thin, whispery voices.

"Friend of Faeries!"

"Great Heart, Great One."

"Basil the Brave."

"Dragon Unrivaled."

"Wings of Peace."

Names, he realized. *They're giving me names.*

His massive lips curled upward. "No need to give me new names, my friends. I am simply Basilgarrad—and I am always glad to help you."

The faeries' whispers swelled, now more like a gust of

wind than any form of language. He could no longer make out their words. But he couldn't mistake their adoration.

At last, the blue cloud started to dissipate. The faeries departed, leaving Basilgarrad's face. Their wings now moved more relaxedly; the flock seemed to be floating rather than flying.

He watched them go, hardly stirring as he glided over the scorched terrain. Cocking his huge ears, he strained to hear the last of their soft, whispery voices.

Those voices reminded him of someone else, a dear friend who moved with the grace and constancy of the wind itself. For she was, in fact, a wishlahaylagon—a sister of the wind. She had traveled far with him, and always called him "little wanderer" . . . even after he'd grown into a mighty dragon. But finally the day came when, like the wind, she had to move on, and nothing could convince her to stay.

His ears trembled slightly as he wondered, *Where are you now, Aylah? In this world . . . or some other?* The ears swiveled. *Dragons are too big to miss anyone. Certainly anyone as flighty as you! But I suppose I wouldn't mind hearing your airy voice again, or catching your cinnamon scent on the breeze.*

A whiff of sulfurous smoke, belching from a volcano below, made him cough. And brought him instantly back to the present. Who could ever stay for long in a realm that smelled so bad? Time to return to the sweet glades of Woodroot!

As he raised his wing, banking a wide turn, he caught a

final glimpse of the departing mist faeries. With a rumble of amusement, he said, "Wings of Peace? Not half bad, really. Not half bad."

Then, with a mighty slap of his wings, Basilgarrad headed for the wooded realm he called home.

3: AN EXCELLENT TIME TO DO IT

A good sleep—such a treasure, it shouldn't be wasted on the weary.

Curling his gargantuan body into a circle, Basilgarrad filled almost the entire bowl-shaped valley. This had long been one of his favorite places to sleep—partly because it held no trees, so he wouldn't be tickled by their trunks snapping under his weight. And partly because it lay in the deepest forest of innermost Woodroot, a place so remote that he wouldn't be disturbed. Except, of course, by Merlin—who could find him anywhere.

As his lids drooped, covering the bright green fires of his eyes, he produced a smell of marsh lilies and pond water—one of his most favorite, most soothing aromas. Soon the scent of lilies filled the air, and he sighed contentedly.

He thought back over the experiences of the day. His battle with Lo Valdearg, that murderer who had dared to take the name of Basilgarrad's own father, the most powerful dragon of ancient lore—and who couldn't contain his hunger for the dwarves' flaming jewels. His conversation with young Ur-nalda, who couldn't believe that he had once been small, even smaller than she. His brief encounter with the dactylbirds, and the grateful embrace of the mist faeries.

None of these things, he reminded himself, could have possibly happened before he changed from the scrawny little creature he'd been to the gargantuan one he was now. Life was entirely different these days! *And yet . . .* he mused, *most of the time I still feel the same down inside.*

He yawned, showing his cavernous, tooth-studded mouth, as his eyes closed completely. Sleepily, he thought about one more experience of the day: a minor scuffle with an ogre he'd met on the way home, somewhere in the western reaches of Stoneroot. The hairy fellow, who had body odor as repulsive as his manners, had developed an annoying habit of ripping the roofs off houses. Before eating all the people inside.

When Basilgarrad stopped the ogre from destroying yet another house and warned him to leave quietly, the fellow didn't exactly respond well. He tore off an especially big roof and threw it at Basilgarrad. So what else could the dragon do but throw this nuisance all the way to the next realm? He'd heard, a few seconds later, a distant thud combined with the squelch of mud—or, perhaps, the ogre's body.

Yes, he thought, drifting into sleep, *it's been a big day. Nothing unusual, though, for a dragon. Especially one who's called . . . Wings of . . .*

He snored, making a gentle, soothing sound that could

have easily been confused with a landslide slamming down a slope or a tornado crashing through a forest.

At that instant, he heard a voice, clear and loud. Not in his ears, but in his mind. He snapped awake, opening his eyes and growling angrily at the sound that had so rudely interrupted his slumber. Yet even as he did so, he knew that all his growling wouldn't help.

For this was the voice of his friend Merlin—a good wizard, mind you, but someone with no sense at all about when to call telepathically. Wizards, unfortunately, have horrible manners.

"Basil!" called Merlin, sounding a bit out of breath. "How are you, old chap? Hope I didn't disturb you."

"Not at all," the dragon thought grumpily. "You merely wrecked my first good sleep after—"

"Glad to hear it," interrupted Merlin. In the background, something exploded violently. "Er, I just wanted to say, old chap . . ."

"Say what?"

Blaaamm! Another explosion echoed in the dragon's mind, followed by the unmistakable sound of something sizzling.

"Just wanted to say," Merlin went on, "that if you'd like to"—*Blaaamm!*—"save my life . . ." The wizard paused while something crackled and something else slammed into the ground. "Er, Basil . . . this would be an *excellent* time to do it."

Having given up on sleep, the great green dragon shook his head. "In trouble again, are you? Where this time?"

"The upper reaches of Fireroot, near the"—*Blaaamm! Blaaamm!*—"gobsken fortress. In the midst of erupting—"

"Volcanoes, I know." Basilgarrad sighed. "Back to Fireroot! Just my luck. Sweet Dagda, I hate that smoky realm."

"You'll come then, old chap? I'll be glad to see you. And so will"—*Ssss-zzzaapppp!*—"Hallia."

"Hallia?" Hearing the name of Merlin's wife, the dragon stiffened. "She's there with you?"

"She is, though not—" The rest of his words were drowned out by an explosion.

"Right." The dragon lifted his head out of the valley, stretching his wide wings. "Just try to stay alive until I get there."

"Will do my"—*Kablaaamm!*—"very best."

Glancing up at the stars overhead, Basilgarrad noted the location of the brightest constellation, seven stars in a straight line known as the Wizard's Staff. Since the very creation of Avalon, those stars had radiated powerfully, guiding night-time travelers. They had also inspired many years of speculation about what, really, were the stars of Avalon: Were they other worlds, or perhaps something more mysterious? But tonight he had no time for speculation. Trouble had erupted—once again. And this time, he felt sure, Merlin couldn't just dismiss it as "growing pains."

His green-tinted tongue pushed against the gap in his

teeth, souvenir of his first real battle. This time, he knew, there would be no magic-eating kreelix to fight. Who would it be, then?

"All right," he declared. "Time to fly."

Taking his bearings, he stretched his neck due east— toward Fireroot. With several powerful beats of his wings, he rose out of the valley. His long, sinewy form lifted toward the stars, as gracefully as smoke from a candle flame.

4: FOR THE GOOD OF ALL

When you think of life as a meal, and imagine yourself as the chef in total control—that's usually when you get cooked.

Flying by the light of Avalon's stars, Basilgarrad beat his wings so fast they were just a blur of motion. No creature could fly more swiftly than a dragon—and he was a dragon in a hurry. A great hurry.

"Merlin," he grumbled as he streaked across the sky, "for someone with such awesome powers, you certainly have a knack for getting into trouble!"

His eyes, glowing green in the night, narrowed. Those troubles had been growing more frequent, as well as more dangerous. For both Merlin and Basilgarrad. And also for the world they loved, a place unlike any other. Avalon—the magical world within a tree, grown from a seed planted by Merlin himself.

It was a seed, the dragon knew well, that had held something more than a new and wondrous world. Something, in its own way, even larger—and even more remarkable. An *idea*. That somewhere in the wide universe, there might be one place where all creatures of all kinds could find a way to live together in harmony. To share their world with mutual respect. To draw strength, rather than conflict, from their differences. And to protect the many beauties of these realms.

The Avalon idea, Merlin liked to call it. It was a notion that stirred the heart as well as the mind. A notion that seemed increasingly at risk. Which was why, despite all his grumbling, he was glad that Merlin had called—as the wizard had recently been doing more often. So often, in fact, that Merlin was spending much more time with Basilgarrad than with his wife, Hallia.

Basilgarrad roared, even as he flew at dragonspeed. There was only one place he wanted to be—a place that had seemed impossible for the tiny little fellow of his youth, a place that now felt more like home than anywhere on the land. *By Merlin's side.*

Looking below, his great scaled wings beating steadily, he recognized each of the seven root-realms. Soon after leaving Woodroot, whose forests smelled so fresh and sweet, he spied Waterroot—where seas gleamed, even in starlight, with all the colors of the rainbow. A few moments later: Stoneroot, whose bells he could hear chiming at any time, day or night. Now Mudroot, whose soil Merlin had enriched with the magic of life. Next came Airroot, called Y Swylarna by the sylphs, where he could see the layered clouds that were the dancing grounds of the mist maidens. In the far distance—the eternal darkness, blacker than black, that was Shadowroot. And now, just below him, the volcanic realm of Fireroot.

He veered north, toward the mountainous terrain where

the gobsken had recently built a fortress of stone so thick that even dragons' fire could not penetrate. Despite their antipathy toward the gobsken, for whom fighting was as natural as breathing, Merlin and Basilgarrad had decided to let the fortress stand. So long as the gobsken didn't use it as a base to conquer other peoples, no problem. And if the gobsken's long-standing feud with the fire dragons kept those two groups busy battling each other, the fortress could be a useful distraction. Was it too much to hope that this ongoing feud could occupy the dragons so fully that they would forget about their obsession with the dwarves' flaming jewels?

Passing over a line of volcanoes, Basilgarrad searched for any sign of Merlin. Through the sulfurous fumes and eruptions of boiling lava, he spotted a troop of marching gobsken. A field of sizzling hot lava pools. A forest of dead ironwood trees, their trunks and branches blackened by flames.

But no sign of the wizard.

He turned slightly, skimming over the craters of an old volcano. The fetid clouds that clogged the air made his eyes burn, but he stared at the fire-scorched terrain. Something about those craters didn't seem right. Almost as if . . .

There! Topping a ridge on the volcano, he spied a new eruption of flames. But this wasn't the fire of molten lava. No, it was the fire of *dragons*. A whole circle of them, directing their deadly flames at one person who stood in the center.

Merlin!

Standing on the rim of a crater, the wizard hurled blasts of lightning from his staff and golden balls of fire from his free hand. Constantly whirling and spinning, while dodging the attackers' blasts of flame, he looked more like a dancer than a warrior. But this was no mere entertainment. He was fighting for his life.

Seventeen, eighteen, *nineteen dragons!* Basilgarrad's mind whirled. How could one man, even a wizard, have held off such an overwhelming force? And how should he, as the lone dragon on Merlin's side, best help his friend?

He slowed his flight enough to scan the scene as he drew closer. Lit by the flaring volcanoes as well as the stars above, the attackers showed all the colors of Fireroot's dragons: red, orange, and amber. And yes—among them was a huge scarlet dragon Basilgarrad recognized.

Well, well, Lo Valdearg, he said to himself. *Feeling strong enough already to fight again?* He snorted, nostrils flaring. *How unlucky for you.*

Focusing on the wizard, Basilgarrad noticed right away that Merlin's face looked unusually haggard. His thick black beard had been singed, the hem of his cloak torn. Suddenly the dragon saw, hidden inside the crater, another figure.

Hallia! Though he recognized her, this huddled figure barely resembled the woman who had won Merlin's heart long ago, whose grace and kindness and ability to transform herself into a deer were famous throughout Avalon. Wrapped in a tattered blue shawl, she leaned against the crater's rock wall, dodging stray bursts of sparks and flame. Her auburn braid was coming apart; her eyes, as large as a doe's, were filled with fear.

Something stirred within the crater and moved toward her. Another person! Basilgarrad strained to see through the volcanic haze—then recognized who it was: Krystallus, the son of Hallia and Merlin. In recent years, he'd grown into a strapping young man. As tall as his parents, with a mane of pure white hair, he seemed quite regal—despite the fact, to Merlin's disappointment, he showed no sign of magical ability. As the dragon watched from above, Krystallus took his mother's hand, trying to comfort her.

Basilgarrad then noticed something else about the crater. It held, in its center, a cluster of green flames—not the fire of battle, but the same magical fire that burned in his own green eyes. The fire of élano, the most powerful magic of all, the essential sap of the Great Tree of Avalon.

A portal, he realized in awe. Here in the remotest part of Fireroot! Had Hallia come here through that portal? Surely Merlin wouldn't have brought them here intentionally—to this scorched wasteland where no one lived besides warlike gobsken and wrathful dragons.

Just as he shifted his wings, preparing to land, Basilgarrad understood why the craters on this ridge seemed so odd. Unlike the craters he'd seen elsewhere, they were perfectly round. Circular—as if they'd been . . .

Carved, he realized. Hollowed out—by people with the skills and tools to do so. People such as dwarves!

In the final seconds before touching down, he put it all together. *These aren't craters, after all. They are entrances! To the dwarves' underground tunnels. Maybe even to—*

Before he could finish the thought, he saw Merlin deflect a new, terribly fierce barrage of flames from the dragons. *Time to announce my arrival*, he decided—and landed with a thunderous crash, slamming into the blackened ridge right next to the crater.

The force of his impact nearly toppled Merlin from the crater's rim, but the wizard managed to steady himself with his staff. Instantly, all the surrounding dragons halted their blasts of flame. In that moment of silence, the eyes of Merlin and Basilgarrad met.

"What took you so long?" asked the wizard, his voice gruff but affectionate.

"Oh, I took in some of the sights on the way." Then the dragon's eyes narrowed with concern. "What's your plan?"

"Plan?" Merlin scowled. "I thought *you* would have a plan."

"Green dragon!" boomed a powerful voice from the ring of attackers. "Whose side do you choose?"

Basilgarrad spun his massive head around to face the speaker—an enormous dragon whose orange scales were almost completely blackened by soot. Columns of smoke poured from his nostrils; rage burned in his amber eyes. Though one of the largest dragons in the ring, he was still only two-thirds the size of the green dragon who had appeared so suddenly. Standing beside the orange dragon, Lo Valdearg started in surprise. Then he grimaced in rage. Smoke curled from his nostrils, and he angrily clawed at the remaining charred stubs of his beard.

"Which side?" demanded the orange dragon. "That of your brethren, the dragons of Rahnawyn?" He blew an especially dark puff of smoke. "Or this ragtag wizard who tries to keep us from our jewels?"

"*Your* jewels?" called Merlin, his voice booming nearly as forcefully as the dragon's. "They belong not to you, but to the dwarves! Who are, even now, underground as I instructed them—but who would bravely answer your attack if necessary. You do not own the jewels just because you crave them as a mosquito craves blood."

"Soon we shall!" Sparks of flame flew like spittle from the orange dragon's mouth. "Just as we dragons will soon control every part of this realm, crushing any foes who stand in our way."

By his side, Lo Valdearg nodded and glared at one foe in particular, the only dragon who had ever defeated him in battle.

The orange leader thumped on the ground with his foreleg, sending up a cloud of ash. "Choose now, green dragon, for tonight's battle begins anew. And before it is over, any allies of that wizard will be dead."

From within the crater, Hallia said something to Merlin, too quietly for anyone else to hear. The wizard frowned grimly in reply.

Moving his vast bulk slowly, Basilgarrad raised his tail into the air. All of a sudden, he brought the tail's clubbed end down with a resounding crash. Rocks and dirt and ash flew skyward. Vibrations shook the ridge like a powerful tremor.

Three or four of the dragons in the ring lost their balance, rolling into their neighbors. As the explosive sound faded away, he spoke—not only to the orange dragon, but to everyone in the ring.

"I am Basilgarrad." From deep in his throat came a terrible rumble. "And I stand with Merlin."

Instantly, the orange dragon—joined by Lo Valdearg and most of the others—shot a barrage of superheated flames. Basilgarrad swung around, protecting the people in the crater with one wing and his eyes with the other. But he didn't retaliate. Not yet.

As the withering volley of flames subsided, he raised his head high. "Is that all you have?" he taunted. "Nothing more?"

Another blast of flames erupted—strong enough to melt the black rock of the ridge, forming sizzling rivers of obsidian. But once again, Basilgarrad's wings deflected the fire. When at last the onslaught ceased, he lifted his head again. Surveying the ferocious dragons, he declared, "Flames you have, my cousins. Flames and power! But I ask you—what good are they? Are such great gifts worth no more than this, to spend them on lives of thieving and murdering? Is there no greater calling for dragons, the most wondrous creatures in any realm of any world?"

He paused, letting his words hover on the night air. Lowering his voice to a deep rumble, he asked, "Why not use your great power for something else, something more worthy? Why not use them for the good of all?"

A few of the dragons, including Lo Valdearg, snorted with

contempt or laughed out loud. But Basilgarrad's steady gaze did not waver. Over on the crater, Merlin nodded in agreement, while Hallia and Krystallus poked their heads above the rim to watch.

"I ask you, fellow dragons," continued Basilgarrad, "what is a life of conquest but an empty egg? If everything you own has been stolen from others or ripped from the land, what value have you created? True value—and yes, true greatness—lies not in what we take, but what we give."

Surprisingly, a few of the dragons looked anxiously at each other. Another few, feeling the sting of his words, cocked their heads in thought. A small but growing murmur of uncertainty began to rise around the circle.

"Ignore that treachery!" Lo Valdearg's voice thundered, echoing on the volcanic ridges around them. As the largest dragon in the ring—even bigger than the orange leader, though still smaller than Basilgarrad—he spoke with commanding authority. All the other dragons turned his way. "For treachery it is."

Emboldened by the vastly superior numbers on his side, Lo Valdearg took a few steps forward. Facing the green intruder who had dared to challenge the dragons' ways, he roared, "You are nothing but a tool—a pet of that wizard over there. He controls your life, not you! And a dragon should be free. Or he is not really a dragon at all!"

Almost all the dragons around the ring nodded their heads. Several banged their huge tails against the ground, thumping their approval.

Looking straight into the intruder's eyes, Lo Valdearg sneered, "You dishonor all your kind. Look at you, green pet! Why, you can't even breathe fire."

Several of the surrounding dragons grunted in surprise. Though only Merlin noticed, Basilgarrad himself winced ever so slightly.

"That's right," Lo Valdearg went on. "He may be big, but he's still just a Green from Woodroot. He couldn't light a little campfire, let alone make a powerful blaze. No wonder he preaches peace—he's not fit for war!"

Without warning, the scarlet dragon blew a raging breath of fire straight at his foe. So great was the hot blast that Merlin was nearly blown over backward into the crater. But Basilgarrad did not retreat. He merely turned his face away momentarily and took the full force of the attack on the scales of his neck and chest. When the flames died down, he slowly turned back to face Lo Valdearg.

"You really are stupid." Basilgarrad shook his head. "Even more stupid than you look. And that's nearly impossible."

At that, Lo Valdearg blew another searing blast at his face. At the same time, he charged with frightening speed, aiming to sink his teeth into any part of Basilgarrad's body. If only one of those teeth cracked a scale—that would be a grievous wound.

Simultaneously, the orange dragon called to the others, "Help Lo Valdearg! Vanquish the enemy!"

Heeding the command, every dragon in the ring rushed

forward. Teeth bared, they blew a torrent of flames. So fast did they move, they were on their enemy in a flash.

Not fast enough, though. Basilgarrad spun away from Lo Valdearg with surprising speed, then did something completely unexpected. Bracing his immense body, he whipped his mighty tail—and wrapped it around the scarlet dragon's neck. With a deafening roar, Basilgarrad used his enormous strength, along with Lo Valdearg's momentum, to lift the other dragon off the ground. He whirled his foe around and around, clearing the circle and using the bully's body as a shield.

Lo Valdearg, taken by surprise, could only release a strangled gurgle from his throat. The other dragons, pushed back by this huge whirling club, gazed on in fear and astonishment. No dragon in history had ever done something so bold in battle!

"Kill him! Rush him!" commanded the orange leader. "You cannot be defeated by a single dragon."

His soldiers, however, wavered. Only a handful of them charged, and each met with a painful slam by the whirling body. Two were struck so hard in their heads that they toppled over, unconscious. And still Basilgarrad's tail kept spinning.

"Charge him, you fools!" The orange dragon shouted louder than ever, spraying sparks from his mouth. "Charge him now!"

Just then, Basilgarrad arched his broad back and lifted his tail straight up—and with it, the helpless dragon who had become his weapon. Using all the strength he could muster, he brought down Lo Valdearg—right on top of the exasperated leader.

The colliding dragons shrieked, while bones cracked and scales splintered. When all the clouds of ash finally cleared, Lo Valdearg lay sprawled upon the body of his leader. Moaning in pain, he rolled off and slammed to the ground. The orange dragon, whose back had been broken, never moved again.

Confused, distraught, and thoroughly frightened, the other dragons scattered in all directions. They leaped into the air and flew away as fast as they could, not daring to look back, lest the bold green dragon decide to pursue them.

At the scene of the battle, Basilgarrad surveyed the remains of the attackers. Just beyond the crushed corpse, Lo Valdearg, unable to fly, crawled away in anguish. After watching him for a few seconds, Basilgarrad delivered the most humiliating blow of all: He simply turned away.

Swinging around to face Merlin—who, along with Hallia and Krystallus, gazed at him with grateful admiration—the green dragon narrowed his eyes. With gusto, he declared, "Let that be a warning to anybody who dares to call me a pet."

5: FLAMES

Words are like knives. They can spread butter and honey—or pierce a beating heart.

Peering over the crater's rim, Basilgarrad glanced at the portal's mysterious flames, so like the green fire of his own eyes. Those flames could magically transport anyone around Avalon almost instantly—a dangerous way to travel, but very useful for creatures who weren't lucky enough to be able to fly at dragonspeed. This particular portal had, apparently, brought Merlin's wife and son to this fire-blackened realm. But why?

"Oh, Basil," said Hallia, her doe eyes full of gratitude. She lay her hand on the crusty black pumice of the rim. "You were marvelous. Truly marvelous."

He raised his enormous clubbed tail, then let it slam back to the ground, sending up ashen clouds on every side. "Fighting is just one of those skills you pick up," he said modestly. "Of course, it helps if your opponent has a brain the size of a speck of dust."

"You didn't have just one opponent," countered Krystallus. He shook his head vigorously, which made his long white hair—so unusual in such a young man—swish against his shoulders. "You had nineteen! And you bested them all!"

"That's right," agreed Merlin. He tore some tattered shreds of cloth off his sleeve and threw them aside. "That kind of fighting skill isn't something you just pick up. It's a rare gift that—"

"I wasn't talking about his fighting!" interrupted Hallia. She climbed a step higher on the rim to be a bit closer to the dragon's face. Though her whole body could have fit inside the pupil of his eye, she gazed at him confidently, as his equal. "No, something else entirely."

"Not his fighting?" asked Krystallus, bewildered. "Then what were you talking about?"

"His *words*." Hallia continued to peer straight into the enormous green eye. "*True greatness*, you said, *lies in what we give*." She beamed at the dragon. "That was marvelous."

Lowering her voice, she added, "It doesn't matter at all that you can't make fire in your belly . . . when you can make such fire with your words."

Basilgarrad's eyes blushed slightly.

Merlin, standing atop the rim, grinned at the dragon. "Better watch out, old boy, or you'll find yourself an adopted member of the deer people."

Hallia gave his leg a shove. "We'd be honored to have him. Especially since the last person we adopted was a clumsy young wizard with a terrible habit of getting into trouble."

"Well!" the wizard replied, feigning insult. "That description of me is entirely out of date. Now I'm a *fully grown* wizard with a terrible habit of getting into trouble."

Her doe eyes, usually so warm, seemed to freeze over. "Not only with dragons," she scolded. "Right now you're in trouble with *me*."

Merlin's face fell. He averted his eyes, as if he felt guilty about something. Turning back to her, he started fumbling for words—something Basilgarrad had never seen him do before.

"My love, I know that—I, well, you . . . ah, well . . . you must understand. But no, of course you don't! Not yet. Just let me . . . I've been wanting to, ah, tell you, but—no, no, not here! Not now."

"Why not?" she demanded, her gaze still icy. Like an impatient deer, she stamped hard on the ground.

Merlin waved his torn sleeve, making it flap in the air. "Because it's . . ." He glanced over at his son, and then at the dragon looking down at them. "Private! That's why. It's private. Between you and me." He reached out his hand, hoping to take hers. "I promise you, as soon as we have time—"

"Time!" she said frostily, pulling away from him. "That's what we *don't* have anymore. Time together. It's gotten to the point I have to beg Krystallus to take me through a portal just to see you—and then only until the next crisis takes you away!"

Merlin cringed visibly, and Basilgarrad felt a sharp pang of sympathy for his friend. But something inside the wizard seemed to snap. His expression suddenly changed from guilty to angry. Very angry. But instead of exploding at Hallia, he directed his rage at Krystallus.

"You never should have brought her here! Don't you know how dangerous portalseeking can be? How could you risk your mother's life that way?"

The young man scowled. "I know about portals! More than you, probably. Don't talk to me like I'm three years old."

"Hard not to, when you act like—"

"Stop changing the subject!" broke in Hallia, stamping her foot again.

"The subject is your safety," retorted the wizard.

"No, it's not."

"It is!" Merlin twisted his staff into the ashen ground, grinding its tip forcefully. Turning back to his son, he declared, "Risk your own life, if you must—traveling all over Avalon, for whatever reasons. But not someone else's! And especially not *hers.*"

"What would you know about my reasons?" The young man's fists clenched, turning his fingers almost as white as his hair. "When I was small, you never cared, and when I left home early, you never even noticed."

Both his father and mother winced at those words. But Krystallus merely shrugged, as if none of that mattered anymore. "The fact is, I love exploring. Finding new places. Drawing the first maps. What's wrong with that? What's so irresponsible about exploring—compared to abandoning your family?"

Hallia touched his shoulder. "Wait, now. That's too strong."

"No, it's not." Krystallus glared at his father. "He cares a lot more about his work—those chances to show his famous wizardry—than he does about either of us."

Silence fell over the group. Except for the crackling flames of the portal, and the occasional skittering of a pumice pebble that rolled down the volcanic ridge, no sound could be heard. Basilgarrad watched his friends with dismay. And with growing frustration: He had no idea how to stop this argument, and no idea where it might lead. For the first time in a long while— only a few moments after he had vanquished an army of dragons—he felt totally powerless.

Merlin was the first to speak again. To the dragon's relief, his voice was calm, even kind. "Look, son," he began, search-ing for the right words, "I know I haven't . . . been much of a father. I suppose . . . I thought, when you grew up, we could find—"

"When I grew up!" spat Krystallus, quaking with rage. "Once you decided I didn't have any wizard's magic, you forgot all about me. Not that I care! Just don't pretend you ever wanted to be a real father."

Merlin staggered, nearly losing his balance on the rim of the crater. His complexion, lit by the flickering flames, whit-ened again with anger, and his eyes flashed. "I could have done better, that's certain. But I didn't have much material to work with."

Ignoring Hallia's gasp, he added, "You never showed any sense. Never! Which is why you think nothing of trying to impress your mother by dragging her through a deadly maze of portals, right into a battleground."

"I didn't drag her."

"You could have killed her! Portalseeking isn't child's play. Surely I at least taught you that!"

Krystallus stared at his father. In a voice as hard as iron, he said, "You never taught me *anything*. Except how to be a terrible father."

Hallia bit her lip, glancing from one of them to the other.

Merlin's eyebrows, thicker than brambles, lifted. "And you never taught me anything except—"

"Stop," cried Hallia. "Say no more!"

But her husband ignored her. "How to be a miserable son."

Krystallus slowly sucked in his breath. Then, without another word, he spun around and strode straight into the green flames of the portal. A loud crackle split the air—and he was gone.

Basilgarrad slowly shook his gargantuan head. How, he wondered, had the evening's victory turned so quickly into defeat?

Hallia drew her blue shawl closer, as if a chill wind had blown through the desolate lands around the crater. She looked up at the stars for a few seconds, hoping to find some guidance or, perhaps, some comfort. But the deep lines on her brow showed she had found neither.

Merlin, meanwhile, stared into the shimmering flames that had just swallowed his son—and any chance of an ongoing relationship. Slowly, his coal-black eyes lowered, until he was gazing morosely at his boots.

Hallia turned to him and snapped, "You foolish, foolish man! Don't you know that he's become one of Avalon's boldest explorers? That he's been through more portals than even Queen Serella of the elves?"

The wizard frowned. "No . . . I didn't know. I've been too—"

"Busy, yes, I know." She snorted.

Defensively, Merlin grumbled, "I still say it was reckless to bring you here! Even if you did ask, he should have known better. Why would he do such an idiotic thing?"

She strode closer. "Don't you see, you brainless oaf? By bringing me all the way here, he was trying to impress someone—the person whose opinion matters most."

"You, of course."

"No!" She glared at him. "*You*. His father."

Merlin looked into her face, genuinely taken aback. "Me?"

"How else, without any magic of his own, does he prove himself?" Her voice dropped to a quaking whisper. "How else does he make himself worthy of being the son of Merlin?"

The wizard didn't answer. He merely turned and gazed into the restless, shape-shifting flames.

6: MAGICAL SPARKS

Learning a new language is easy—even the underwater words of mer folk, or the whistle-speak of cloud faeries—compared to learning how to raise a child differently than you were raised yourself.

Two weeks later, Merlin and Basilgarrad sat together by a crackling campfire in the Volcano Lands region. Although these flames were markedly different from the green fire of the portal where he'd argued with Krystallus, the wizard watched them with the same silent despondence, lost in his thoughts.

The dragon, meanwhile, lay stretched between a row of small volcanoes. Whenever one erupted, spitting an annoying fountain of superheated lava into the air, he merely rolled over and crushed it. How else to make it keep quiet? Unfortunately, the lava usually found its way to one of the other volcanoes, making it necessary to smother that one, as well. This continued well into the evening, as the realm darkened around them. Eventually, Basilgarrad sighed a deep dragon's sigh: Volcanoes could be so pesky! Yet another reason he didn't like Fireroot.

As Merlin's friend, he knew that it was pointless to try to

coax the wizard to talk before he was ready. During the entire time since that debacle with his son, Merlin hadn't spoken about it—except to Hallia. Soon after Krystallus's departure, the married couple had taken a long (and, judging from their faces when they returned, tearful) walk together. Then, after a somber embrace with Hallia, Merlin asked the dragon to take her where she wanted to go—to one of her favorite haunts, a rolling region of meadows and glades in the heart of Woodroot that the deer people called the Summerlands. When Basilgarrad returned, the wizard only wanted to talk about work—and suggested they might try to craft some sort of truce between the fire dragons and the dwarves. Although Basilgarrad could sense that there was something else troubling Merlin, something much bigger than this feud in Fireroot, he could also sense that the wizard still wasn't ready to explain.

In time, he told himself. *He'll tell me in time.*

Alas, their efforts to arrange a truce had failed miserably. Hard as they tried, they couldn't even start a conversation with the fire dragons. Whenever Merlin appeared by himself, the dragons only wanted to battle him to the death. And whenever he appeared with Basilgarrad, they instantly fled into hiding.

The attempts to talk with the dwarves proved no more productive—for different reasons. While expressing their heartfelt gratitude to Merlin and Basilgarrad for rising to their defense, the dwarves clearly didn't like the idea of sharing their labors—or their wealth—with the greedy dragons. They listened skeptically as Merlin described a possible treaty where the dragons might do some of the heavy work needed to excavate underground, and melt down ore with their fires, in exchange for some of the jewels that would be mined. But no sooner had Merlin finished speaking than a voice boomed loudly, "Bah! We might just as well give them all our treasures right now."

The wizard knew that voice well: It belonged to Zorgat, chief elder of the dwarves, someone Merlin had hoped would see the wisdom of his words. The old dwarf, whose silver beard stretched down to his boots, stood as still as stone, arms crossed on his chest. Not even the dwarf raven pacing on his shoulder, occasionally nibbling on his ear, distracted him. He merely stared grimly at Merlin.

"My friend Zorgat," the wizard had replied, "won't you at least—"

"No," the dwarf declared, cutting him off. His eyes, the same silvery hue as his beard, glinted like the facets of jewels.

Merlin protested, "Won't you even consider this idea?"

Zorgat scowled, tugging on his silver beard. All at once, he reached over his shoulder and pulled an arrow out of his quiver. He held it in his hand, twirling it, watching the black obsidian arrowhead gleam darkly.

"Peace," he said, "is only possible when two people see their destinies as one—bonded like the head and feathers of an arrow."

Merlin nodded, suddenly hopeful.

Zorgat suddenly grasped the arrow with both his gnarled hands and broke it over his knee. Peering straight at the wizard, he tossed the two broken halves aside. "Where there is no bond, there can be no peace."

All around the elder, dwarves grumbled in approval and stamped the ground with the heads of their battle-axes.

For a long moment, Merlin gazed right back at the old dwarf. Then he strode over to the spot where the two pieces had landed. Picking them up, he carried them back to Zorgat, and placed them at his feet.

"When the time comes that you are ready to think anew, to try to end this violence, send me this arrow—with the shaft repaired."

"Merlin," the dwarf replied, "that will never happen."

"You have lived long enough, my friend, to see the wisdom of my words. And to see some things happen that no one would ever have believed possible."

The elder grunted. "Still, this will never happen. *Never.*"

Dwarves being thoroughly stubborn people, that had ended the meeting. But it hadn't, by any means, ended the concern that Basilgarrad could see etched on Merlin's face—concern that ran deeper than dwarves and dragons.

And so now . . . Merlin and Basilgarrad sat together by a campfire's crackling flames. The stars of Avalon, bright as ever, had begun to emerge. But Merlin's mood could not have been darker. He sat on the ground, leaning his back against the dragon's lower lip, occasionally tossing magical sparks into the campfire.

Basilgarrad, for his part, occupied himself making diverse smells—the more bizarre, the better. This served both as entertainment and as a way to obscure the heavy, sulfuric odors of the volcanoes. So far he'd managed to produce the aromas of bubblefish popping, acorns roasting, a mudslide congealing, a field of purple mushrooms going stale, and lightning striking an overweight frog.

Hmmm, he thought, savoring the scent of scorched frog. What an enjoyable—and totally useless—pastime! Was there any reason, other than entertaining himself on a night like this, that he'd been given the unusual power of casting smells?

Rolling his body just enough to squash another irksome volcano, he concluded, *Maybe that's reason enough.*

Merlin hurled another spark into the flames, then glanced up at the dragon's immense snout. "You know, Basil . . . I'm worried."

The dragon remained quiet and still, even resisting the urge to squash another spray of lava. This was the moment he'd been waiting for. And he wanted to give Merlin whatever time might be needed.

"Very worried," the wizard continued. "About the plight of the weaker creatures we've been helping—more and more often recently. Dwarves, mist faeries, lilac elms, and the rest. And also about the rise of the stronger creatures we've been battling: fire dragons, dactylbirds, ogres, and shape-shifters."

He drew a long, slow breath, absently toying with a magical spark on his fingertips. He flicked the spark onto the back of his hand, then rolled it across his knuckles. "But the truth is, Basil, I'm even more worried about something else."

"Which is?"

"Avalon." Merlin threw the radiant spark into the campfire, watching it sear a sizzling arc through the air.

The dragon's enormous eyes opened wider. "I thought you considered these battles mere nuisances—*growing pains*, you called them."

"Early on, I did. Then, as they gathered momentum, I started to worry. More than I wanted to admit. To myself, let alone to you or Hallia. But that near-disaster two weeks ago—when we had to fight not just one errant dragon, but a whole army of them—well, that confirmed my worst fears."

Basilgarrad's huge tail thumped the ground, causing a small landslide on the nearest ridge. "Fears for Avalon."

"That's right, my friend." The wizard's tufted eyebrows drew together. "Our world, as you know, is unique—a thoroughly unlikely experiment, a testing ground for bold new ideas. Can all these diverse creatures live together in peace? Can all these wondrous places survive forever? That's what Avalon is about, nothing less."

He leaned forward, taking his weight off the dragon's jaw. For the first time, he turned to peer upward, straight into the huge eye above him. "And, Basil . . . I fear the experiment is starting to fail."

The dragon released a rumble from deep in his throat. "Why? What is happening?"

"I don't know! I'm still not even sure this isn't just a co-incidence, a time of random troubles with no greater meaning. Like a season of heavy rains."

"These rains, though, bring death."

The wizard nodded grimly. "All I am sure about is that I've been traveling constantly, through all the realms, trying to keep the peace. You've been doing the same, I know—though I've tried to spare you as much as possible. That's why I only call you for emergencies."

"Which happen now every day," replied his huge companion.

"So it seems." Merlin struck his fist against his knee, which caused a spray of sparks to burst from his knuckles. "This is a crucial time for our world. Our idea. If Avalon can get a good start, get through this, this . . . *rainy season*, then it could live forever! Our experiment could succeed! And if not . . ."

He shook his head, letting his dismal expression finish the point. "That is why, Basil, I've been calling on you so much recently. And why I've been traveling constantly—even when I knew my long absences were painful to Hallia. The stakes are just too high."

Drawing a slow breath, he added, "She understands now, at least in her mind. But I'm not so sure about her heart."

"I suppose," said the dragon with surprising gentleness, "that when it comes to matters of the heart, even a wizard has a little to learn."

"More than a little." Merlin flicked some new sparks at the campfire, watching them sail through the air and land in the crackling embers. "Just look what a good job I've done with Krystallus."

"You can't blame yourself for—"

"Yes, I can, Basil. The truth is, I've done to him exactly what my father, Stangmar, did to me. And what his father, Tuatha, did to him. I've pushed him away—probably for good."

The corners of the dragon's mouth turned downward. "It's too bad, really, that he didn't inherit some of your magic. Then you would have had more to share as father and son."

Merlin scratched his black beard thoughtfully. "No, that's not it." He twirled an especially long hair. "The problem wasn't *his* lack of magic. It was *my* lack of confidence. You see . . . I always feared I'd do as badly as my own father did with me. So I stayed away, worried that if I spent too much time with him I'd do the wrong thing. And now I see what folly that was! I ended up doing exactly what I wanted to avoid."

For a long moment, neither spoke. Volcanoes spurted occasionally, illuminating the night air, while the campfire sizzled and crackled. At last, the wizard found the words to continue.

"What I understand now—too late to help Krystallus—is that magic comes in many forms. Some are simply harder to see than the more obvious ways of wizards and dragons."

"You mean . . . like his skill at navigating portals? It's a rare gift that you could, I suppose, call magic."

"You could," answered Merlin, "but I mean something

even more subtle . . . and mysterious. The way a seed sprouts into a tree. The love between two people. The light that sparkles in the wings of a butterfly, or the eyes of a child. Those things, I would say, are the essence of magic."

"And you would be right." Basilgarrad thumped his tail again, crushing one of the smaller volcanoes into a smoking pile of cinders. "Magic is all around us—in every seed, every leaf, every person."

Merlin nodded, forming a spark in his hand. He peered at it, rolling it from his fingertip down to his palm, before tossing it into the campfire. The spark glowed bright for a few brief seconds as it sailed through the air, then vanished in the flames. Quietly, more to himself than his friend, he repeated, "Every person."

At that instant, Basilgarrad caught sight of something strange. Just at the edge of his vision, a tiny creature moved, edging toward a cracked volcanic rock. A leech! The small black worm—with twisted folds of skin, a circular mouth, and a lone dark eye—crawled lazily across the ground.

That's odd, he thought, having never heard of any leeches in this region. What was here for them to feed on? Baby dragons, perhaps, whose protective scales hadn't formed? Or gobsken's eyelids—the only part not covered with bony skin? Or maybe the flamelon people—though they lived far east of here, by the mouth of the River of Fire.

The dragon suddenly caught his breath. For the sight of that leech—an annoying but harmless little beast—reminded him of something not at all harmless. Something he had, in all his adventures as a dragon, allowed to slip to the back of his mind. Something that both he and Merlin, caught up in their lives, hadn't talked about for years.

Rhita Gawr. The wicked spirit warlord, always hungry to conquer Avalon, had smuggled a bit of himself here years ago, disguised as a leech. A leech that possessed its master's dark magic . . . and equally dark purpose.

When Basilgarrad, then still very small, first discovered it, the leech looked like any other, a black worm identical to the one he'd spotted just now. Except for one important difference: The creature of Rhita Gawr had a blazing, blood-shot eye.

All this flooded the dragon's mind as he watched the little beast edge away. As it disappeared behind the cracked rock, he suddenly felt a bit silly. Why should he worry about such things? Nobody in Avalon had seen any further sign of that evil leech, in all this time. Nobody. More than likely, the beast had died—shriveled up for lack of someone's blood to suck.

And besides, he said to himself with a satisfied grunt, *if I defeated that little pest when we were practically the same size . . . why should I worry now that I'm a dragon?*

Down in his massive throat, he chortled. *And a rather big dragon, at that.* To be sure, he was now even bigger than Shim, that ludicrous but well-meaning giant. Bigger than his sister dragon, Gwynnia, who—along with her aggressive offspring—had once made such sport with him. Bigger even than the famous water dragon, Bendegeit, who, according to the bards, was so huge that he could sink a ship with just the flap of one ear.

With that, he turned to Merlin. The wizard had gone back to staring into the campfire, lost in his thoughts.

Meanwhile, hidden from view behind the rock, the leech stopped moving. Slowly, it straightened, standing upright like a tiny twig. Then it did something most unusual. From the depths of its dark eye, it released a series of bright red flashes, as if it were sending a signal to someone else.

When the flashes ceased, some of the red light lingered. Only for a few seconds—but long enough to transform the source of light into a blazing, bloodshot eye.

7: A Rising Tide

Who ever said misery loves company? I like to have my misery all alone, the way I like to have a hunk of meat: no company, no conversation, just me and something raw to chew on.

The green flames crackled loudly, parting like a curtain as a lone hand reached through, grasping at the moist air. The hand surged forward, followed by a lean, muscular forearm, and a sturdy shoulder. Then came a head that, while belonging to a virile young man, was crowned in pure white hair.

Krystallus stepped forward, emerging from the portal. He stood on a small, uninhabited island covered with sand dunes and woven braids of latticeweed. Standing straight, his hands upon his hips, he looked out at the beach strewn with blue and gold sea stars and shreds of kelp—and at the enormous expanse of blue sea beyond. Taking a deep breath, he filled his lungs with briny air, so laden with salt it tasted almost like a hearty meal.

"Brynchilla," he said, exhaling. Wherever he traveled, he always preferred the local names of places. Brynchilla, the elven term for *realm of water*, seemed much more poetic than the Common Tongue's name, Waterroot. Even if it had been coined by his despised competitor, the elf queen Serella, the name suited this place, fitting it as smoothly as a wave fits upon the shore.

Scanning the horizon, an uninterrupted expanse of blue sea that merged seamlessly with the lighter blue of the sky, he pulled his sketch pad from his tunic pocket, opened its rippled leather cover, and did what he always did upon arriving anywhere in Avalon: He drew a map. In seconds, the lines from his favorite osprey quill pen—which he'd dipped into a vial of octopus ink—filled the page, revealing the island's contours, the shape of the horizon, as well as the portal's location, wind and ocean currents, and visible signs of life.

As he sketched the map, he nodded grimly. He knew where he was, though he'd never discovered this particular portal before: in the remotest waters of Brynchilla. And, more importantly, he knew where he was *not*. This island was just about as far away as anyone could get from that volcanic fire pit called Rahnawyn. Yet his memories of that place, and the bitter fight with his father, still felt all too near.

His heart raced angrily. How could his father be considered so wise, yet really be so foolish? How could he have so little faith, so little confidence, in his own son? Both his hands clenched as he thought again about their parting words—most likely the last words they'd ever speak to each other.

"Fine by me," he muttered, squeezing his fists. "I don't care if I never see him, let alone talk to him, again!" He had his own life, his own goals, not least of which was to create a whole college devoted to mapmaking and the exploration of

Avalon. And that life had nothing whatsoever to do with his father. He could easily spend all his time exploring the farthest reaches of the world—which had been, since childhood, his greatest passion.

A briny breeze blew over the sea, tousling his hair. It stroked his face and parted the collar of his simple brown tunic, as if offering an invitation. At once, Krystallus knew what he wanted to do most in this watery realm.

Swim!

Quickly, he stowed his sketch pad, untied his belt, threw off his tunic, and kicked his leather boots into the sand dune behind him. Wading into the water, he felt the sudden slap of liquid coolness on his legs. His skin tightened; his toes grasped the slick, algae-coated stones underfoot.

Into the water he plunged, feeling the cold embrace on his arms, shoulders, and face. He emerged with a splash, spraying water all around, sucking in a lungful of air. Then he floated on his back, his arms and legs gently swaying. Long strands of white hair radiated from his head like slender shafts of sea kelp.

Peering up into the hazy blue sky, he tried his best to discern the stars. No luck. They lay hidden behind their own daytime radiance, invisible until evening starset. Strange, he thought, how less light makes them more clear, while more light washes them away.

Waves gathered upon the ocean of his brow. "There is a pathway up there, I know there is! All the way up the trunk and branches of the Great Tree—all the way to the stars."

The water buoyed him, bouncing his body gently. But Krystallus didn't notice. "Someone, someday, will find that path," he mused. "Someone, someday."

A pair of snowy terns dove out of the sky, skidding to a splashy landing not far from his head. Droplets sprayed his face. Breathing deeply, he smelled the sweet dew on their wings, carried perhaps from the Flowering Isles, where colorful water lilies bloomed constantly.

Turning to the side, he caught a glimpse of an emerald green shadow gliding just beneath the surface. A porpoise? A sea turtle? An azure-winged water butterfly?

Looking closely, he turned his attention to the water itself. The same cool liquid that, even now, slid under his arms and tickled the small of his back held more colors than just blue. Many more. For this ocean held rivers of rainbows. Greens, violets, even scarlets and golds, coursed through every wave. Interwoven streams of color flowed all around him, trembling and shining in the light.

The Rainbow Seas, he said to himself. *How rightly named!* A wave washed over his face, but he barely noticed. For he himself had chosen that name, on his very first voyage to this realm. Just as he'd chosen the name *Wellspring of Mist* for the enormous tower of spray that rose out of the ocean not far from here. Like a gargantuan fountain, the Wellspring lifted into the clouds above like upside-down rain.

Feeling much calmer inside, if a bit chilly from the water, he turned over and swam back to shore. As he emerged, dripping wet, another breeze flowed past, drying his back and arms and legs. He shook his mane, sending scores of drops across the sand. Grabbing his tunic and belt, he donned them quickly, then sat down to pull on his boots.

"I do love to swim," he said to the dunes and the sky and the endless sea. "Almost," he added as he tugged a boot onto his wet foot, "as much as I love to travel."

His sharp eyes caught a row of unusually tall waves that rose from the horizon as sharply as peaks. No—not waves. Sails! The sails of ships.

Elven ships, he knew, recognizing them now. They must have sailed from their bay to the south. Bands of elves from El Urien's forests had come there with their leader to establish a new colony, called Caer Serella. *And a new breed of elves, I would guess, after enough time passes. Wood elves no longer— they'll someday be water elves.*

He watched the ships skimming over the waves with the speed of the wind. Their giant sails taut, the boats leaned far on their sides, practically flying through the water. Already he could see the shapes of their hulls, lined with giant paua shells that sparkled with iridescent blue, lavender, and green. And there—that emblem of Serella's, painted on all the sails made from woven elbrankelp: a great blue wave set within a circle of forest green.

"Serella!" he cursed, raising his fist at the line of ships. "You may have gotten to this realm first. But there are many more places in this world—more than you've ever imagined. And I will beat you to the best of them."

Realizing that he was, once again, scowling, Krystallus

pursed his lips. Why did that elf queen irk him so much? What was it about her that made his blood boil? The haughty look of superiority on her elegant face, perhaps. Or the way she trumpeted her discoveries, as if there were no other explorers in Avalon. Or maybe . . . the sheer delight she took in sneering at him whenever their paths happened to meet.

"Well, well, if it isn't Krystallus, the amateur explorer?" she had said at their last encounter, a chance meeting at a portal in northern Malóch near the dangerous cavern called Hidden Gate. "Aren't you known far and wide as"—she had paused at that moment, savoring her next words—"as the *son* of somebody famous?"

His scowl deepened, as if he'd never known the tranquillity of a swim. Then slowly it began to fade, as a new idea came to him, replacing anger with resolution, filling his mind as a rising tide fills a bay.

"Serella. Father. Everyone else who mocks me. I'll show you all! I'll"—his dark eyes glowed with determination—"find places and pathways that no one, not even Dagda, knows about. Face any dangers. Solve any puzzles. And make myself indisputably the greatest explorer this world has ever known."

Slowly, he lifted his gaze skyward. "And one day, one glorious day, I'll find a route all the way to the stars."

For a timeless moment, Krystallus stared at the sky, feeling the depth of his resolve. And then he did something he hadn't done in a very long time.

He smiled.

8: ELIXIR OF DEATH

Funny thing about surprises, especially deadly surprises. They are always ready for you—even if you aren't ready for them.

Far, far away, in the uppermost reaches of Malóch, a deadly marsh fumed and bubbled. Many a creature had wandered there by chance, only to meet a violent, horrible death—ripped apart by hungry predators, driven to insanity by the strange lights and eerie sounds that permeated the foul mists, or drowned in the putrid waters by dreaded marsh ghouls.

Especially at night, the Haunted Marsh—as it was aptly called by wandering bards—reeked of death. For at night, when the choking fumes blocked all but the frailest glimmer of light from the stars, the marsh ghouls roamed freely, floating invisibly over the decaying peat and bubbling waters. Even those creatures fated to live in the marsh, who found its vile swamps more habitable than the surrounding arid desert lands, hid themselves away at night.

Or else . . . they died. Slowly, painfully, and horribly.

Night always seemed darker here, as well. Darker than any other place in Avalon, save perhaps the eternally lightless realm of Shadowroot, which for some mysterious reason had never been touched by the glow of stars. Yet night in this marsh wore an extra cloak, woven from threads of fear and grief and despair. That cloak blocked out hope as well as light, making the night seem darker than dark.

On this particular night, nothing stirred beyond the gaseous fumes, the flickering lights, and the moaning forms of the marsh ghouls. Except for one shape—a strange form that had come, years before, to the most remote and repulsive part of the marsh: a deep, ragged pit where the ghouls had long piled the decayed remains of their victims. Filled for decades with the anguished corpses of creatures who had been drowned, beaten, and drained of life, this pit reeked not merely of death, but of the collective anguish and terror of all who had died.

Deep inside that pit, the strange shape moved slowly and deliberately. If anyone had been there to watch, something would have seemed very wrong: This shape could actually be *seen*, even in the darkness of night.

How could that be possible? Not because the shape emitted any form of light. No, quite the opposite.

This shape emitted a deeper kind of darkness. Not merely the darkness of night, nor the rich black that was the color of ebony or obsidian—this was the complete *absence* of light. The ultimate darkness of the void.

The shape belonged to a being that was, in fact, alive. Darker than anything else in the Haunted Marsh, it resembled a shadow of a shadow. A gap in the night. A hole in existence.

Now, standing upright in the bottom of the wretched pit of death, the sinewy being swayed slowly from side to side. For it was drinking, gorging itself on the substance that fed its growing body and fueled its growing power.

Blood? No, this being had long ago abandoned drinking mere blood—although it had, in its early days when it resembled a common leech, sucked all the blood out of many unsuspecting victims. Many of them had unwittingly carried it closer to the marsh, closer to its goal of this reeking pit. And some of those victims had tried, unsuccessfully, to thwart its plans.

One of those creatures, a mighty stag who was the mortal form of the god Dagda, had foolishly carried it all the way to Avalon from the spirit realm. That stag had even lost some of its blood, rich in magic, to the leech's unending thirst. It writhed angrily, remembering. For if its plans hadn't been spoiled by a miserable little lizard—who had somehow grown into a dragon—the stag would surely have died. Not from loss of blood, but from the toxic poisons that only a very special kind of leech could produce.

A leech who was, in truth, the servant of Rhita Gawr.

Now a gigantic leech, taller than a fully grown man, the spirit warlord's agent in Avalon was drinking a substance much more vile, and much more powerful, than blood. It was filling itself with the misery, horror, and anguish of this forsaken place. By feeding on those ingredients—the very elixir of death—it would eventually grow stronger than any mortal being. Yes, including a dragon! So strong, in fact, that its master could finally enter Avalon and make this world his own.

For now, though, the shadow leech lived for only one goal. To consume whatever suffering it could find. To drink from the bounty of death in this marsh. And when that ran out, to cause even more suffering and death—so that it could continue to drink and drink and drink some more.

That was why, when it had grown powerful enough to spawn, it began to produce its own minions. Difficult as it had been to make them, it had managed to spawn exactly seven of them over the years—one for each root-realm of this world. The minions, each resembling a common leech, had been dispatched to the realms and commanded to send back the essence of any pain and suffering in their midst. And to do whatever possible to encourage more misery.

Only a few moments before, the minion in Fireroot had used its dark magic to convey an unusually satisfying potion made from some family's rage, frustration, and regret. Something about that potion had tasted familiar, somehow, to the shadow leech. Tantalizingly familiar. But it didn't have the energy or time to spare pondering why.

It needed to drink. And grow. And prepare itself for its next, truly magnificent, feat.

The being of darkness swayed a bit more vigorously, sucking up all the anguish in its midst. For the very thought of that next feat made it quiver with anticipation. Yes . . . that feat would enable it to grow much faster, multiply its powers, and open the gate at last for Rhita Gawr's conquest of Avalon.

And one thing more. That next feat would truly justify the name it had taken for itself—a name that meant, in the language of the spirit realm, *darker than dark*. A name that would soon, in this world, be synonymous with death.

Doomraga.

Again, the shadow leech quivered. A deep red glow, throbbing like a wound, appeared at the top of its shape—the being's bloodred eye. Then, from the infinite blackness of its body, came a blast of freezing cold wind, chilling even to the marsh ghouls. That wind carried even more chilling words:

"Doomraga. Darker than dark."

9: THE WHOLE BRIDGE

Learning how other people speak their language? That's easy.
But learning how they think and dream—that's hard.

Wings outstretched, the enormous green dragon soared on a powerful swell that spiraled ever upward. Here he was, high above the shifting clouds of Airroot, where vaporous shapes glided serenely in all directions. Basilgarrad's thoughts, though, were anything but serene. Like the wizard who rode atop his head, holding the edge of a cavernous ear with one hand and a gnarled staff with the other, the dragon felt increasingly troubled.

Things weren't going well in Avalon. Merlin's worst fears were coming to life. Quarrels, attacks, and thievery were happening more often, in every realm. Take, for example, Fireroot: Despite the amazing victory over the orange dragon and Lo Valdearg—a victory the bards had already dubbed the Battle of One Against Many—skirmishes between fire dragons and dwarves hadn't stopped. On the contrary, they had grown more frequent. And more savage.

"If only," Merlin grumbled, turning his face into the great

ear in order to be heard above the whistling wind, "old Zorgat had given my idea a try!"

Beneath the wizard, Basilgarrad's brow furrowed, causing the wind to whistle across his scales. "Wouldn't be like the dwarves to seek common ground with their enemies, would it?"

"No," Merlin admitted, as they passed through a multi-layered veil of mist. "But with all the people they've been losing, whether to these skirmishes or mine collapses—which the broad backs of dragons might have prevented, if they were working together—even old Zorgat must be wondering."

Basilgarrad banked to the right, skimming the edge of a huge cloud covered with thousands of misty pinnacles—Airroot's famous Forest Afloat. Just below the dragon's wing rose the translucent spires of eonia-lalo trees, whose bark is almost invisible. If not for the flocks of chattering birds—doves, owls, sparrows, cormorants, terns, and others—resting in their branches, the trees would have seemed like one enormous mass of mist.

"Something else is happening," Merlin continued grimly, while the dragon flapped his great wings and leveled out again. "Something I can't quite identify."

"I know," came the dragon's reply, echoing around the clouds.

"Remember when I said we'd entered a *rainy season*? Well, Basil, that was the right image. It feels more rainy every day."

"No," said Basilgarrad with a shake of his head—which Merlin didn't appreciate, since it threw him right into the dragon's ear. "It's more like those rains have turned into floods! Terrible floods." And then, to emphasize his point, he shook his head again—just as Merlin was climbing out of the ear, sending the wizard tumbling back down again.

"Something worries me even more than the floods themselves," Basilgarrad went on, oblivious to the wizard's current troubles. "It's a feeling I can't shake—that something is *causing* them. Encouraging them. Linking them. Do you agree?"

"I don't know," panted Merlin, climbing back up to his perch. "But whatever you do next, don't shake your head!"

The dragon rolled one eye upward, peering at him quizzically. "What's gotten into you? You sound as irascible as that marauding troll we beat back to his cave last week."

Rather than try to explain, Merlin just growled. Then he said, "That's an example, though. Stoneroot's trolls, big and stupid as they are, have never caused that kind of trouble before. What made that one so angry? He seemed absolutely *driven* to wreak havoc."

"I hope a few months alone in his cave—with that pile of boulders I put at the entrance—will be enough to cool his temper."

"So do I." Merlin brought his staff over to his face, as wind flapped the sleeve of his tunic. Using the staff's handle, he brushed aside some hairs that had caught on his bushy eyebrows. Then, scowling, he said, "And what about that band of gnomes we dealt with yesterday? Wasn't it strange how angry their leader was, screaming and waving his spear all the time?"

"Strange, yes," replied the dragon. "As was something else."

"What?"

"Did you notice how *pale* he looked? His face and the rest of him, now that I think about it, was drained of the gnomes' usual color. But he had no wounds, no reason for blood loss, as far as I could tell."

"Hmmm, maybe—" Merlin began, then caught himself. Pointing below them, he declared, "That's it, Basil. Our next problem, the one the sylphs told me about." Under his breath, he added, "Let's hope it's easier than the last few."

Tilting his mighty wings, Basilgarrad swooped down toward the place Merlin had indicated. As the clouds shredded around them, affording a clearer view, he saw the latest source of trouble. To his surprise, it was a bridge—a span of roughly woven white ropes that connected two large, lumbering clouds.

"Those ropes," explained the wizard, anticipating his question, "are made from a solid sort of cloud—cloudcake, the sylphs call it. It's the strongest substance in this realm, strong enough to support—"

"A bridge," said his gargantuan steed, the deep voice full of wonder. "And look! All those birds sitting on it—black crows on the left, white terns on the right."

He paused, taking in the scene. The birds were making a

raucous din, screeching and cawing angrily. Every few seconds, a bird from one side would fly across to the other side, beat several other birds with its wings or poke them viciously with its beak, then fly back. Often two or three terns descended on a crow, attacking with beaks and claws until they were finally beaten back—though not before they had drawn blood. Just as often, a group of crows played the same brutal trick on a tern.

Merlin, holding tight to the dragon's ear, leaned forward for a better look. "Strangely, those birds have been quite peaceful, according to the sylphs. Until recently."

Basilgarrad tilted his wings, gliding lower. "Another flood, then. Just why are they there, anyway?"

"When the bridge was built, years ago, those birds started guiding creatures across. It's been especially helpful to all the cloudbound beings—vapor possums, mist monkeys, and the like—who couldn't otherwise cross through so much open air. And the birds came to love their work, calling themselves *the bridge guides.*"

"So why are they fighting?"

The wizard shook his head. "Despite all their years of working together, they've suddenly chosen sides. The terns want no one but terns on their half, while the crows want no one but crows on their half. Now nobody can cross anymore! And mark my words, if we don't calm those tensions soon, this bridge will be soaked with blood."

Basilgarrad heaved a dragon-size sigh. Stretching his wings

to their widest, he glided closer. As they neared the bridge, he heard another sound, audible whenever there was a lull in the birds' angry chatter. "Harp strings?" he asked, bewildered. "Are those harp strings I hear?"

"Yes, indeed, Basil. You are hearing the sylphs' finest creation: titanic harps, strung between the clouds. They're many leagues from here, but their sound travels across the cloudscape. And their strings are moved not by winds—but by *emotions.*"

The dragon's ears swiveled in surprise, nearly knocking Merlin off balance. "So they respond to whatever emotions are around?"

"That's right. Which is why, right now, they sound so horrendously out of tune."

As if to emphasize the point, the harp strings played an especially jarring series of notes.

Because he couldn't possibly land on the bridge—those spans would have snapped under his weight—Basilgarrad sailed slowly over the spot. Suddenly noticing him circling, the crows and terns ceased their feuding and fell quiet. For exactly two seconds. Then they erupted in louder, more hostile cacophony than before—each side accusing the other of treachery involving a dragon. The screeching, hooting, whistling, and cawing rose to a terrible level.

Merlin leaned over the side of Basilgarrad's brow. "Silence!" he commanded in the Common Tongue, waving his staff above his head.

But the birds paid no attention. If anything, their angry din swelled even louder. In the distance, the sylphs' harp strings jangled vigorously.

"Silence!" he commanded again. But the noise was now so loud that his words couldn't even be heard, let alone obeyed.

Basilgarrad, circling above the birds, frowned at their bad behavior. His voice no louder than a typical thunderstorm, he bellowed, "Quiet, all of you! Or I'll blow off all your feathers."

Instantly, the birds fell silent. But for the occasional nervous rustling of a wing, they made no sound whatsoever.

Rolling his eyes up to Merlin, the dragon said with satisfaction, "Someday I'll teach you how to do that."

"Please do," said the wizard, clearly impressed. Then, drawing in a deep breath, he added, "Now, just watch how I settle this mindless dispute.

"Birds of the realm," he began, "I understand you have a serious grievance. True?"

Hundreds of heads bobbed vigorously, as the birds showed unanimous agreement. A few of them started to screech and clack their beaks with anger—but before the noise could start to swell, Basilgarrad cleared his throat menacingly.

At once, silence returned.

"And I understand," Merlin continued, "that half of you—the crows—want to control one half of the bridge, while half of you—the terns—want the other half. Is that true?"

Again, many heads bobbed. And twice as many eyes anxiously watched the dragon gliding above them.

"Well, then," announced Merlin with finality, "I have the solution to your problem." He waited for a moment, allowing the birds' anticipation to build. Then, with a flourish, he declared, "From this day onward, each of your kind shall control half of the bridge. You terns—" He waved to the left. "That half. And you crows—" He signaled the right. "That half."

The birds nodded and clucked with agreement. Merlin, watching, allowed himself a grin.

"That means," he went on, "that no tern shall ever trespass on the crows' side, and no crow shall ever cross to the terns' side."

Again, all the birds nodded.

"And that also means," he concluded, "that each of you may only guide creatures across your own half of the bridge. When you reach the middle, you must take them back to where they started."

Out of habit, many birds started to nod in agreement— then caught themselves. As the meaning of Merlin's plan sank in, more and more birds started to shake their heads or flap their wings in protest. A few, while still eyeing Basilgarrad, squawked loudly.

The dragon himself sent the wizard an urgent thought. "What are you doing, Merlin? That would just make this problem worse!"

The wizard's grin expanded. "Just wait, my friend."

"No, we won't do it!" a young tern declared. "We are *the bridge guides*—not just half-guides."

"To do our jobs," called a crow, "we need to cross the whole bridge."

Dozens of other birds joined the chorus. While the voices were each different, their message was the same: The bridge must be shared.

"Are you sure?" asked the wizard, sounding reluctant. "Quite sure?"

"Yes!" cried the birds, louder than ever. But this time their voices were mostly unified.

"All right, then," said Merlin with a shrug of his shoulders. "Have it your way."

Together the birds released a sustained cheer of whistles, clucks, trills, and cries. In the distance, harp strings played melodious, soothing chords. The entire bridge swayed with jubilation.

Basilgarrad, much impressed, exclaimed, "Bird psychology! How did you know how to do that?"

The wizard's expression turned wistful. "I had a friend once, a hawk." He glanced at his left shoulder, where the feisty bird often perched. "He taught me a great deal."

Meanwhile, the birds' noisy celebration continued. Only one bird, a rather bony crow, screeched in protest and flew away angrily. No one noticed that, in the feathers of its neck, an unusually bloated leech sucked greedily.

10: A Colorful Visitor

What blows your way on a breeze, I've learned, is usually some kind of trouble.

Satisfied that his ploy had changed the attitude—and community—of the bridge birds, Merlin leaned forward on the dragon's head, listening to the pleasing sounds of cooing voices and fluttering wings mixed with the distant melodies of harps. Wind rushed past his face, blowing his hair backward and parting his beard; he seemed, for the first time in weeks, truly relaxed. Basilgarrad, lazily circling above the cloudcake ropes, felt equally content. Then he glimpsed, at the edge of his vision, something strange.

Out of the hazy center of a shredding cloud, a smaller, silvery cloud approached. Beneath the small cloud hung a suspended shape—a round object, deep purple in color. But what kind of object could it be? And why was it coming this way?

The dragon peered at it closely. Suddenly, he realized what, and who, it was. The purple object was a person—an especially grumpy one named Nuic. As a pinnacle sprite, he showed his emotions in the colors of his skin (which accounted for the angry shade of purple). And the cloud carrying him was no cloud at all, but a parachute made of silvery threads he could sprout at will.

"Well, well," said Merlin, who had also caught sight of the approaching visitor. "If it isn't that merry little fellow Nuic." Whispering into the dragon's ear, he added, "I don't know what Rhia sees in him, but at least he's loyal to her."

Riding the wind, the round-bodied sprite glided swiftly toward them. Now they could easily see the arch of his eyebrows and the frown on his face. When he came within earshot, Merlin called out, "Always a pleasure to see you, Nuic."

The sprite, tugging on the strings of his parachute to steer closer, maneuvered himself to a gentle landing on Basilgarrad's head. As he drew the parachute back into his body, pulling the strands into a gap between his shoulders, he glared up at the wizard.

"Hmmmpff," he said gruffly. "The pleasure is all yours, believe me. I only came because I need to talk with you."

"About what?" asked Merlin, wrapping his arm around the ear of the dragon.

"I'll tell you when I'm ready!" shot back the sprite. "Have you no manners at all? Before we talk, you should introduce me to your scaly friend here."

"Right," said the wizard sarcastically. "I forgot all those manners you taught me." Clearing his throat, he asked, "Have you met my friend Basil?" He waved his staff at the dragon's broad wings and enormous tail. "We often travel together."

"My sympathies to both of you." Nuic's color darkened to muddy brown. "But, no, we have not met before."

Basilgarrad released a deep, throaty chuckle that expanded into a booming laugh. The sound of his merriment echoed around the surrounding clouds, a joyful form of thunder.

Nuic strode over to the edge of the massive brow and demanded, "What's so funny, dragon?"

"We *have* met before," came the amused reply. "You just don't remember."

Nuic's chest showed plumes of orange amidst the brown, a sure sign of confusion. "Really? How could I not remember meeting someone as big as a mountain with a warped sense of humor?"

Basilgarrad's eyes flamed brightly. "Because, master sprite, when you met me I wasn't as big as a mountain. I wasn't even as big as your puny little fist!"

Nuic shot a harsh glance at Merlin. "Does he hallucinate like this often?"

"Maybe," suggested Basilgarrad, "this will remind you."

All at once, the air filled with the revolting smell of carrion and murderous claws. Nuic's color instantly turned white. He darted to Merlin's side, crying, "Dactylbirds! They're here!"

Once again, the dragon's resounding laughter filled the skies. Merlin, too, joined in, laughing so hard he almost let go of Basilgarrad's ear.

It took only a fraction of a second for Nuic's color to change from white to purple mixed with swirls of fiery orange. "Not—not y-y-you!" he sputtered. "Not that rude and sassy little mystery beast who can make annoying smells?"

Basilgarrad's lips curled upward, revealing several gleaming rows of teeth. "That's right, old fellow. I've changed a little since you saw me last."

"B-b-but . . ." Nuic clearly couldn't fathom this dramatic shift. The purple hues deepened. At last, he muttered, "I liked you better before."

The dragon snorted. "And before, you wanted to kill me."

"Hmmmpff," said Nuic, his color turning a more urgent shade of red. "Are you two buffoons going to spend all day bantering? Or is someone going to ask me why I came here?"

Merlin rolled his eyes. "Tell us, please."

From a tiny pouch on his belly, Nuic drew a small brown leaf. Some sort of disease had gnawed at its edges, making the leaf woefully ragged. Only the thinnest hint of green remained at the base of its stem. Several of its veins had darkened to black, while others had crumbled completely.

"Recognize this?" he asked Merlin.

"No," said the wizard, puzzled. He took the leaf in his hand, examining its frail edges, its blackened veins. "But it's clearly in trouble. Serious trouble."

All at once, he started, crumpling the leaf in his hand. "Why, it's Rhia's! From her suit of woven vines." He bit his lip. "Basil—take us to her now!"

11: THE BLIGHT

All good things must end, the saying goes. Why, though? Why must something truly good finally perish? I resent that idea. Yes, and I stand against it, with all my heart.

Slicing through the clouds, Basilgarrad beat his mighty wings. With every powerful stroke, he brought his passengers, Merlin and Nuic, closer to Stoneroot. For there, at the circle of stones in the heart of the Society of the Whole's compound, they hoped to find Rhia.

Wind whistled across the dragon's scales, seeming to shriek the word *fffaaasssssster*. No creature in Avalon could fly so swiftly. But would it be swift enough?

Merlin, holding tight to the dragon's ear, looked grim. He leaned into the wind, willing his friend to fly even faster. For Rhia—who was, to the rest of the world, the Society's High Priestess—was, to him, something much more precious: his sister and dear friend. Only Hallia and Basil came as close to his heart.

He swallowed, thinking about that diseased, crumbling leaf from Rhia's suit of woven vines. She had never, even after their mother, Elen, had died, liked to wear the elegant gown made from spider's silk that signified the High Priestess. No, just as she'd done for many years as a young woman in Druma Wood, she greatly preferred the feel of natural greenery as her garb. Especially since those particular vines carried with them the ancient magic of Lost Fincayra's most wondrous forest. Magic that could survive forever—unless attacked by some poison potent enough to kill the entire forest . . . and maybe Rhia, as well.

If her gown is suffering, Merlin thought, *then so is she*.

We'll get there soon, answered the dragon telepathically. His great wings beat furiously. *Very soon*.

A few minutes later, they spotted the stone circle, whose pillars had been carried all the way from Lost Fincayra in the earliest days of Avalon. Just outside the circle sat the famous Buckle Bell, made from the belt buckle of a giant. Nearby lay several brightly colored gardens, which Rhia and her followers had started to cultivate in honor of Dagda, god of wisdom, and Lorilanda, goddess of birth and renewal. Beyond that stretched many fields of grain as well as dozens of farmhouses, each topped with a weather vane and a bell. The only land around not being cultivated for some purpose was a lumpy, irregular hillside that rose from the edge of the stone circle.

Basilgarrad's brow wrinkled. Landing amidst so many obstacles wouldn't be easy. He much preferred the open plains to the south or wide glaciers to the north. But here was Rhia's home, so here he would land.

Arching his wings, he veered sharply to avoid hitting the hillside or any of the farmhouses. With a thunderous slam, he hit the ground. Merlin and Nuic were thrown forward, rolling down the dragon's snout to land on top of his massive black nose. Several of the largest pillars in the circle of stones wobbled precariously, then fell with a crash onto the hillside.

At that moment, the hillside woke up. Or, more accurately, stirred in its sleep. For it was, in fact, no ordinary hillside. It was a sleeping giant with bedraggled hair, a vest of knitted pine boughs, and a bulbous nose.

"Shim!" cried Merlin, recognizing his old friend. With the help of his staff, he regained his feet. "Shim, wake up!"

But the sleeping giant merely shifted his enormous bulk, barely missing the roof of one farmhouse with his hairy big toe. The stone pillars, which had fallen onto Shim's open hand, didn't fare so well. Between grunting snores, he tossed them aside as if they were nothing more than a few pebbles. Then, settling back into peaceful slumber, the giant mumbled, "Take that, you villainly villain! Certainly, definitely, abs . . ."

Merlin, watching the sleeping giant, shook his head in dismay. Nuic, already a wrathful purple because of the discarded pillars, did the same. Only Basilgarrad found himself grinning, for he couldn't forget his first encounter with Shim. On that day, the huge fellow had also been sound asleep, and in danger of crushing Merlin's son, Krystallus, then just a toddler. Only the piercingly sweet smell of honey, sent by Basil to the giant's nose, caused him to wake up in time.

From behind the rubble left by the collapsed pillars, two people strode toward them. One, a tall priest missing an ear, Basilgarrad recognized as Lleu, a longtime friend of Merlin and Rhia. The other, he was delighted to see, was Rhia herself. She seemed as healthy and vibrant as ever, radiating her usual feistiness, even though the vines of her garb were peppered with sickly brown leaves, such as the one Nuic had brought. Her feet—bare, as she preferred—sprang lightly from the ground; her curls bounced with every step.

Merlin rushed to embrace her. "You're well!" he exclaimed, sighing with relief.

"I am," she declared grimly. "But Woodroot is not!"

Woodroot. Basilgarrad's favorite realm, whose lush, scented forests he called home. What was wrong there? What had happened?

Rhia stooped to pick up Nuic, and gave his arm a grateful squeeze. "Come now, I'll show you. Words can't explain— you must see for yourselves."

Merlin turned to the enormous dragon, who lay sprawled behind him, narrowly fitting between the stone circle and the sleeping giant. "Basil, will you take us?"

"Anywhere," he replied.

"Aim for the headwaters of the River Relentless," Rhia instructed him. "Then go north."

"Must we ride on that oversized lizard again?" grumbled Nuic. But no one seemed to notice—certainly not the dragon, who had already lowered one of his long ears to the ground so his passengers could climb aboard.

Slithering forward so he could open his wings without knocking down any more pillars, Basilgarrad found enough space to take flight. He leaped into the air, banked a turn to avoid clipping Shim's foot, and beat his wings. Westward he flew—toward Woodroot.

Moments later, the dark green border of Avalon's forest realm came into view. Even before he could see much of the wooded hills beyond, Basilgarrad caught some of the forest's familiar scents: spruce resins, both sweet and tart; lilac blossoms, rich with ethereal perfume; bark and wood, wet from rain, melting into soil; acorns, each one holding the essence of an oak tree; and mushrooms, mysteriously savory.

As they crossed into the realm, mound upon mound of greenery rose into blue ridges that wore shadows like thick blankets over their dells and ravines. Spirited streams ran through every fold, splattering and spraying with endless ebullience. Plumes of mist rose from the glades, as did the lilting notes of songbirds. More smells wafted toward them—deer prints in a marsh, ripening plums, peeling birch bark, moistened tufts of moss. Then, from directly beneath them, a flock of lemon faeries lifted into the air, their tiny yellow wings glittering like stars.

"Further north," said Rhia, sitting cross-legged on the dragon's head. Wind rushed through her hair, straightening all but her most tightly wound curls. She glanced to her right, where Merlin stood beside a tall ear. "To the deepest forest."

Lleu, standing by the dragon's other ear, raised his voice to be heard above the wind. "What *was* the deepest forest."

No one spoke again as they sailed swiftly over leagues of rich forest. Trees, all shades of green, filled every contour of the land, just as songbirds' music filled the air. Then, in unison, the companions caught their breath. For the vista before them was starting to change drastically.

Trees, stripped of their leaves, stood like skeletons. The landscape now looked more brown and gray than green, an expanded version of Rhia's dying leaf. Ravines where streams once flowed were sterile and dry; no moss clung to their banks, no fish leaped from their pools. Mist did not rise skyward, only dust clouds stirred by the restless wind.

Basilgarrad strained his eyes, hoping to see some signs of life in this miserable terrain. But the farther north they flew, the more devastated the forest became. Now he saw no loping deer, heard no songbirds, smelled no fruit or flowers.

"What . . . happened?" he gasped.

"A blight," declared Rhia, running her fingers over the woven vines of her garb. Because their magic sprang from the same source as the life of the woods, they, too, were fading. Already, more brittle brown leaves had appeared on her arms, thighs, and chest.

"And it's spreading," said Nuic, seated beside her. His own color had shifted to lifeless gray with a few traces of green.

"What's causing this?" pressed Basilgarrad, shaking his immense head as he flew. To get a closer look, he swooped lower so that his underside nearly brushed the tops of the leafless trees. "What's behind all this?"

"Magic," Merlin declared, his face contorted as if he'd bitten into a bitter fruit. "I can feel it, down in the marrow of my bones. This is dark magic—the worst I've ever encountered."

The dragon veered, following the empty gulley that once

held a stream. The wind, dry and smelling of nothing but dust, rushed over him and all those he carried. It seemed to be blowing away any shreds of hope that the forest might return to life.

"Is there some way to stop this?" asked Basilgarrad. "To counter the magic?"

Rhia, swiveling atop the dragon's head, turned to her brother. "Is there?"

Merlin's dark eyes scanned the wretched scene below. "Perhaps. But it will be very risky."

"It's worth any risk," insisted Rhia. She picked a dead leaf off her arm, then threw it into the wind. Aimlessly, it drifted down to the lifeless forest, landing on the bare ground.

Grimly, he nodded. "So be it. Basil, go farther to the west. Over that ridge there, the one with the notch."

The dragon turned, still flying just above the spiky tree-tops. Seconds later, he crossed the notched ridge. More blighted lands stretched before them, with only a scattering of healthy trees on the horizon.

"There!" cried Merlin, pointing to the left. "Set us down there."

Basilgarrad knew instantly which spot Merlin had chosen. Amidst all the gray and brown below, he saw only one variation—a touch of vibrant green. Not the green of living plants, but of a certain kind of fire.

"A portal," said Lleu, peering down at the flames. "Do you know, Merlin, where this one leads?"

The wizard shook his head. "I know where it *might*

lead—to a place far below the surface of Woodroot, a place we can find only by portalseeking. I've been there once, though only with help from Dagda. But what I saw there was a vast supply of one particular substance—the only substance strong enough to counter this blight."

Rhia's curls bounced as she nodded. "You mean . . . élano?"

"Yes! Not the diluted form we find in healing springs or portal flames. No, I mean pure élano—the most concentrated magic in this world, or perhaps any world."

He twirled his beard, thinking. "I've only begun to comprehend its powers, mind you. But we're talking about the essential sap, the very life source, of the Tree. It combines all seven sacred elements—and the result is, well, magic *beyond* magic."

"And so," said Rhia, suddenly excited, "if we can somehow gather enough pure élano—"

"We might be able to counter the blight," finished her brother. "As strong as that dark magic is, the power of élano just might be stronger. If I'm right, it's a power devoted to creating and healing life, rather than destroying it." He swallowed. "And if I'm wrong . . ." His voice trailed off ominously.

"We lose precious time," finished Lleu. "Meanwhile, this terrible sickness is spreading! If we take too long, there won't be anything left in Avalon to save."

"And we still don't know what's behind all this," the dragon reminded them in his resoundingly deep voice. Descending toward the portal, he lifted his massive tail and tilted his wings. Dusty winds circled as he dropped lower.

"I'll tell you what's behind it," declared Rhia, windblown curls whipping her cheeks. "Rhita Gawr! He wants to end all the life—all the magic—in Avalon. To turn back time, so our world never has a chance to flower. Killing this forest is just the beginning!"

"Now, now," cautioned Merlin. "We don't know that yet. There might be some other explanation."

"Like what?" asked Rhia doubtfully.

He chewed on his lip. "I don't know. Not yet."

She scowled at him. "You always did like to wait until danger strikes you right between the eyes, rather than see it coming! Why can't you call a disaster what it really is?"

"That's what sisters are for."

"To see disasters?"

"Yes," he answered wryly. "Or cause them."

Suddenly Basilgarrad dropped more altitude, preparing to land. Arching his enormous wings, he also lifted his head to protect his passengers from the impact—just as he plowed into a mass of dead trees, mowing them down with his enormous weight. Trunks snapped against his massive chest, while branches exploded, sending shards in all directions. He slid to a stop, then lowered his head once more. Only a few paces from the tip of his jaw, the portal's green fire crackled in the center of a shallow pit.

"Excellent work, Basil." The wizard patted the back of the dragon's ear. "A perfect landing."

"Hmmmpff," grumbled the sprite. "Perfectly horrible, if you ask me. He could have killed us!"

"I'll try harder next time," said the dragon with a smirk.

"There won't *be* any next time," replied Nuic, his skin entirely scarlet.

"Look here," said Merlin, having climbed down to the ground to examine the pit and its flames. His worried tone caught everyone's attention. "This portal, if I'm not mistaken, seems to be frailer than most. See how its fire is sputtering? I wonder if it, too, has been affected by the blight."

"Too bad Krystallus isn't here," offered Rhia, stepping to his side. "He knows so much about the nature of portals, he might be able to tell us."

"Well, he's not here," snapped Merlin. He clenched his teeth, thinking of the bitter parting he'd had with his son. "We'll just have to take our chances."

Rhia eyed him sympathetically. "I'm willing if you are," she said softly. She looped one of her fingers around one of his, as she'd often done since their youth.

Feeling her confidence, as well as her touch, Merlin straightened his back. "All right, then. Shall we enter this portal?"

Rhia, Lleu, and Nuic all gave a nod—although, in Nuic's case, it was barely perceptible. Basilgarrad, for his part, frowned. "I'm too big, I'm afraid."

Merlin gazed up at him. "That's one thing I never thought I'd hear you say."

The dragon's eyes brightened for an instant, then dimmed

again. "This place is somewhere under the surface? I can't fly there to meet you?"

"Right, old friend. I'm sorry."

"So all I can do is sit here and wait for you to return?"

Merlin stroked his scraggly beard. "I never said that." His expression darkened. "There is, in fact, something else you could do. Something that could give us an important clue to what's really happening—not just here in Woodroot, but all across Avalon."

"What is it?" Basilgarrad eagerly pounded the ground with his tail, sending up clouds of dust and debris. "Where do I go?"

"To Waterroot," answered Merlin. "To the lair of Bendegeit, highlord of the water dragons. Now, I must warn you: He is a jealous, wrathful, vindictive monarch, ruthless beyond measure. But he also holds a power that no one else possesses—the gift of Undersight."

"Which is?"

"The power," Merlin explained, "to see beneath the surface, to the true causes of things."

"I will go," vowed the dragon.

"Be careful, though! As hard as it will be to win his help, there will be one thing even harder."

Basilgarrad's ears swiveled. "What is that?"

"To avoid battling him or his guardians." Merlin stepped toward his gargantuan friend. "Water dragons are just as vicious and irascible as fire dragons, I'm sorry to say. The only difference is that, instead of fire, they breathe—"

"Ice," the dragon finished. "Blue ice. I've already learned that—the hard way."

The wizard lifted his bushy brows. "You'll have to tell me about that experience." Lowering his voice, he added, "If we both survive the next one."

"Are you sure that portal's safe enough to travel?" asked Nuic, eyeing the feeble flames.

"No," declared Merlin. "But I am sure it's our only chance."

"Hmmmpff. This sounds like one of your plans, all right! Stay here and die from the blight, or go and die in the portal."

"That sums it up quite well," he answered grimly.

The portal crackled and sputtered like a dying man's cough. Merlin glanced over his shoulder at the flames, then looked again at Basilgarrad. With a nod, he spun around and faced the fire that would carry them to their destination—or their death.

12: GREEN FLAMES

No flame is brighter than hope. It both lights the mind and warms the heart . . . even when there is nothing left to burn but darkness itself.

His face lit by the flickering green flames of the portal, Merlin slid his staff into his belt. With one hand, he held onto Rhia, who carried Nuic in the bend of her arm. His other hand took Lleu's.

"Clear your minds completely," he warned. "Think of nothing but the magical essence élano, lifeblood of the Great Tree of Avalon. And why we must find it—to save our world! Don't let your thoughts stray, for even a second, or you'll die quickly and painfully."

Under her breath, Rhia added, "Or slowly and painfully."

Merlin squeezed her hand. "Stay with me, and you'll be fine. All of you." Yet he didn't sound wholly convinced. "Come now, let's go."

As one, they walked to the edge of the pit. Green fire, sputtering and flaring, lapped at their feet. Merlin glanced to his left and right, then took a deep breath.

"Now."

With that, the companions jumped into the air and dropped into the pit. Crackling flames rose over them—and they vanished.

Green fire overwhelmed them, consumed them—and then, at last, became them. Through the living veins of the Tree they flowed, turning sharply here, falling steeply there, riding deeper and deeper into the inner heart of their world. Onward and inward they rode, carried by the crackling sparks of élano: part light, part life, part mystery.

At some points, the fires dimmed, slowing their journey. Once, the flames nearly faded away, but returned again just in time to carry them onward. Yet there could be no doubt that the portals—and maybe the Tree itself—were weakening.

Throughout, a rich, resinous smell filled their awareness— the smell of the woodland, of trees, of forest life renewing for ages beyond count. That smell, even more than the flames, seemed to be the essence of their journey, the constant re- minder of the fragile beauty surrounding them.

Suddenly, with an explosion of sparks, they tumbled out of the portal onto a floor of solid rock. It took them a mo- ment to untangle themselves and clamber to their feet, and another moment for their eyes to adjust to the dim, milky light that seemed to come from everywhere and nowhere at once.

"Where are we?" asked Rhia. Her voice echoed and reech- oed around them.

"Alive, first of all," said Lleu, straightening his twisted tunic. "And that's a blessing."

"Speak for yourself," grumbled Nuic. Even in the milky light his small body looked very dark.

"We are in a cavern," announced Merlin, "deep under the surface. Whether it's the *right* cavern, I'm not sure." Glancing back at the portal, whose flames sputtered feebly, he frowned. "Let's find out quickly, before that portal dies."

"Leaving us stranded down here forever," added Nuic glumly.

Merlin pulled his staff from his belt and held it before his face. Gently, he blew upon its gnarled handle. Instantly, the staff began to glow like a powerful torch, sending light of its own in all directions.

What a cavern! Huge, arching buttresses, twisted like enormous roots, soared overhead, joining somewhere too high to be seen. All around the companions, smooth rock walls undulated, rising and falling as if they were frozen waves. At the base of one of those walls, the portal's fire burned, spitting green sparks onto the floor.

Yet the light from that fire didn't explain the dim white light they had noticed when they first arrived. It was Merlin who first realized where that light originated. Peering at the cavern walls, he nodded. For there, embedded in the rock, were thousands upon thousands of luminous crystals.

"Crystals of élano," he said in a hushed whisper. "All around us."

Holding his staff high, he strode to the nearest wall. Gently, he laid his open hand against the rock. Milky white light shone right through his palm and each of his fingers, illuminating all the bones and muscles under his skin. The rock felt warm—not only the warmth of heat, a physical sensation, but also the deeper warmth of something spiritual: a sense of belonging to the wide universe, a feeling of contentment, a glimpse of the rhythmic patterns of life.

He turned to Rhia, his face looking younger than it had for many years. Then, as he removed his hand from the wall, his expression turned suddenly somber. "It's here, all around us. But how do we get it? We'd need tools, hammers and chisels, to remove even a fragment."

"Maybe not," said Lleu, stepping forward. As the others looked at him in puzzlement, the tall priest cupped a hand around his one ear. "Listen," he said softly. "Just listen."

All of them stood in silence, trying to breathe a quietly as possible. But for the occasional scraping of a boot or rustling of a sleeve, they heard no sounds at all—nothing but the utter quiet of the cavern.

Then . . . they heard something more. Subtle, delicate, and far away, it was extremely gentle yet unmistakable. *Drip . . . drip . . . drip.*

"Water!" exclaimed Merlin. Smiling, he turned to Lleu and squeezed his shoulder. "Not too shabby."

The priest grinned. "A young wizard I met some time ago taught me that the gifts you're given don't count nearly as much as how you use them."

Rhia moved to Merlin's side. "And where there's dripping water, in a place like this, there might be—"

"A pool," said Lleu. "A pool of distilled élano."

"Exactly." The wizard lifted his glowing staff, sending twisted shadows down the walls. "Let's find out, shall we?"

"Hmmmpff," said Nuic, standing near the portal. "Not to dampen your spirits, but I suggest that, whatever you're about to do, you hurry."

Everyone turned to him—and to the portal. Its flames were fading! Even as they watched, it coughed and sputtered, growing smaller by the second.

"Come!" cried Merlin, running in the direction of the dripping sound. Footsteps echoed throughout the cavern as Lleu and Rhia, who had scooped up Nuic, ran behind him. Shadows flickered across the sparkling walls, as if they were racing against the companions.

Suddenly, Merlin came to a halt. The others nearly plowed into him from behind. Like him, though, they could only gape in wonder at the scene before them.

Everywhere, water trickled from countless crevasses in the walls and dripped from the rootlike buttresses—emptying into a gleaming white lake. Its shining surface stretched before them, on and on, fading into the distance. A lake this size up on the surface would have seemed immense; down here, far underground, it seemed even larger.

"A lake of élano," said Merlin quietly, gazing in awe. "So much magic, so much life."

"And what do you propose to do now, great wizard?" Nuic's gruff voice echoed around the walls, punctuated by the constant sound of dripping and splattering. "Take a drink and hold it in your mouth until we get back?"

"No," he answered, unruffled. "I have a better idea."

Calmly, he strode to the very edge of the lake. Gleaming white liquid lapped against the toes of his boots—and, though no one noticed, several holes in the worn leather magically repaired themselves. Slowly, Merlin lifted his glowing staff, recalling the day he'd first grasped it, fragrant with the scent of hemlock. So dear had the staff become, in the years since that day, that he'd given it a name of its own: Ohnyalei, meaning *spirit of grace*.

Holding the staff upright, he carefully lowered it, so that its tip almost touched the surface of the white lake. Peering at the richly grained wood, as someone would look into the face of an old friend, he started to chant:

> *Hark now, élano, soul of the Tree:*
> *Seek out the magic, the staff Ohnyalei.*

A look of intense concentration on his face, he lowered the tip into the lake. When wood and water met, tiny white ripples expanded from the spot. Swiftly the ripples grew into bubbling, churning froth. The lake seemed to be boiling around the tip, as the staff shook violently in Merlin's hands. All the while, he squeezed the staff hard—so hard his knuckles turned as white as the frothy water.

Finally, the boiling diminished. The water grew calm again, until only a few small ripples remained. Pale and exhausted, the wizard lifted the staff from the water. There, at the tip, gleamed a perfectly formed, seven-sided crystal. It glowed with white radiance, as brilliant as a star—a crystal of pure élano.

Tired as he was, Merlin managed a frail grin. To the staff in his hands, he whispered, "We did it, my friend."

Yet there was no time to admire the magnificent crystal now gleaming on his staff, or to linger at the lake. With a quick glance at Rhia, he turned and started running back down the cavern, although his legs felt as heavy as stone. Panting with exhaustion, occasionally stumbling, he forced himself to move as fast as possible. The others ran with him, footsteps pounding.

Moments later, they reached the portal—just as its last frail wisp of flame sputtered, hissed, and vanished. Where the green fire had burned, there was now just a charred hole in the cavern wall.

For several seconds, the companions could only stare at the dark hole. Merlin swayed on his feet and leaned against Rhia. His eyes darted from the dead portal to the precious crystal they had worked so hard to find. How could they have come so far, only to be blocked from returning home? Now, with a chance to save Woodroot—and the rest of Avalon— from the terrible blight, would they never leave this cavern?

Weak as Merlin was, an idea suddenly sparked in his mind, growing swiftly into a flame of its own. Lifting his staff, he plucked the crystal from the tip. Gently, he set the precious object down on the rock floor, right before the hole where, so recently, magical fire had burned. Then, in a voice barely louder than a whisper, he spoke.

"Please," he said. "Rekindle the fire. Relight the portal."

Nothing happened for an agonizing moment. Then . . . a bubbling, sizzling sound arose from the hole. The smell of forest resins drifted through the air. All at once, the portal crackled and burst into bright green flames.

"Quickly!" cried Merlin. "While it lasts!"

He grabbed the crystal and placed it in his tunic pocket, then slid his staff into his belt. Extending one hand to Lleu and the other to Rhia, who was holding the sprite, he took a deep breath. At the instant their hands clasped, they leaped together into the flames. The fire crackled loudly, swallowing them whole.

Quiet returned to the underground cavern. No sounds echoed among its glowing walls, but for the continuous crackle of flames and the ceaseless dripping of water—sounds that had started when the world of Avalon began.

13: A TASTY LITTLE MORSEL

Eating is one of life's greatest pleasures. Unless, of course, what's being eaten is you.

Basilgarrad watched the flickering flames of the portal after Merlin and the others took their leap. Even in the first few seconds after they left, the green fire seemed to shrink and grow weaker. Like everything else in this blighted part of Woodroot, the portal's life was quickly fading. Already it looked too feeble to transport people very far . . . if it could carry them at all.

Would they survive their quest? Would they find some pure élano, enough to heal this diseased realm—and keep the blight from spreading across Avalon? The dragon's green eyes, dancing with the reflected glow of the portal, narrowed as he considered other questions: Would his own quest to Waterroot fare any better? Would he convince Bendegeit, highlord of the water dragons, to help?

He flexed his long neck and opened his enormous wings. "It's time," he declared, "to fly."

Basilgarrad leaped skyward, and with a powerful beat of his wings, rose into the air. High above the leafless trees, dry riverbeds, and ashen meadows of his beloved Woodroot, he growled angrily. *Whoever is responsible for this will soon answer to me!*

Soaring across the lifeless landscape, he listened to the *crrreakkk* of his scales with each vigorous beat and the regular *whhhoooosh* of his wings. But he heard no other sounds—no crooning songbirds, no chattering squirrels, no wind rustling branches laden with leaves. And instead of the symphony of smells he so cherished in the forest, he smelled nothing but dry dust and dead wood. The force behind such destruction was clearly powerful. And callously evil. How could anyone have done such a thing? And why?

At last, the first hints of new aromas tickled his nostrils. Green leaves—oak, elm, hawthorn, and maple. Then . . . water! Streams of splattering water, their banks lined with moss and rivertang berries. At last, he saw a line of deep green in the distance—the edge of forest beyond the blight. The sight made him sigh with relief. But he knew that those trees, too, were perilously close to death.

His shadow—jagged wings, huge head, and enormous clubbed tail—soon left the gray and brown lands of the blight. As it crossed into the first greenery, Basilgarrad suddenly felt as if he were actually stroking the vibrant trees, touching them with his outstretched wings, feeling their living leaves and needles and flowers.

Now that he was flying over the verdant hills and braided streams of the healthy realm he knew so well, it was almost possible to forget the damaged lands behind. Almost. Yet even as he sailed over uninterrupted greenery, the memory of the blight hovered over the vista like an ominous cloud.

In time, he passed beyond the borders of the forest and entered the thick mist that separated the root-realms. Surrounded by flowing vapors with their own elusive magic, Basilgarrad felt as if time itself was not real, its passage only an illusion. He recalled his brief journey to the Otherworld of the Spirits—and how that world of misty shapes, of realms within realms, had intrigued him. Would he ever have the chance to go there again?

Bursting out of the vapors, the dragon saw below him the upper reaches of Waterroot—High Brynchilla, as the elves called this region. Just below, a great geyser shot fountains of water into the air above Prism Gorge. At once he remembered that, just north of the geyser, grew an enormous field of dragongrass, tasty shoots as tall as trees and prized by many dragons. Especially dragons who, like Basilgarrad, ate more green salad than red meat (although, given a chance, he would gladly splurge on a few fat ogres or a juicy nest of dactylbirds).

Catching the scent of all that dragongrass, so ripe and chewy, he couldn't keep himself from salivating. Or from thinking how hungry he felt.

Swerving in midair, he glided toward the fields. A few good swallows of dragongrass would strengthen him for the journey ahead. Besides, he hadn't eaten for weeks, since he'd drained that sweet-tasting swamp in Stoneroot. There they were now—tall, golden stalks that grew with astonishing speed thanks to the continuous moisture from the geyser.

He landed, swishing through the stalks. Immediately, he opened his jaws and took a huge mouthful. Hints of lemon and clove spiced the moist, chewy fibers. He swallowed, took another bite, and then slid his body forward to take another. In this way, he moved through the field, leaving a wide swath of clipped grass behind him.

After many satisfying mouthfuls, he came to the edge of the field. Beyond lay a large, flat, star-warmed rock. Raising his head, he started. There, napping on the rock, was a family of dragons—a mother and seven or eight partly grown children. And not just any family.

It's Gwynnia. He recognized the mother dragon not by her purple and scarlet scales, nor by her massive barbed tail—but by her rebellious ear that would never lie flat against her head. Right now, since she was dozing on her side, the ear pointed straight up into the sky, like a tree sprouting from her temple. Despite her loud snoring, all her children lay sprawled nearby, sound asleep.

Hard to believe she's my sister, he thought, stretching his neck for a closer look. *Why, she's not even half my size!*

He grinned at the corners of his mouth, recalling how much bigger she'd seemed the last time they had met, at the wedding of Merlin and Hallia. Back then, he wasn't as long as one of her eyelashes. And each of her children was more than a hundred times his size! His grin faded as he remembered how one of those children had pounced on him, mauling and shaking him as if he were nothing but a lifeless plaything.

Only Merlin's intervention had saved him from being ripped to shreds.

Peering closely at the sleeping family, Basilgarrad quickly found the culprit, lying on his back at the far end of the rock. Slightly larger than his siblings, with an orange barbed tail like his mother, he was clearly the one who had attacked so aggressively. There, on his nose, was the jagged scar from the only wound Basil had been able to inflict on him. Just why had he attacked in the first place? The answer to that was simple: He was much bigger than his victim.

Typical bully logic, thought Basilgarrad, wrinkling his snout. Whether it came from an ogre, a dactylbird, or a dragon—it was all the same. And all wrong.

A new idea leaped into his mind . . . and made him chuckle. *Well, well. This might be an excellent time to teach that young fellow a lesson.*

Stealthily, Basilgarrad reached his long neck toward the young dragon, stopping only when his huge head was right above the sleeping body. So massive was Basilgarrad by comparison that the youngster's entire body was covered by the shadow of just one ear. Lowering his head, the great green dragon came even closer, until the tip of his jaw almost touched the dozing fellow's forehead.

Then Basilgarrad did something very small. Very brief. And very rude.

"WAKE UP!" he shouted, in a voice that exploded like a thunderclap above the young dragon's head.

The little fellow instantly came awake. He leaped into the air—but only rose as high as the huge chin above him. Smacking into Basilgarrad's jaw, packed with hundreds of spear-sharp teeth, the young dragon smashed back to the ground, rolled hastily away, and stopped only when his tail became tangled with that of a sibling. At that point, he dizzily focused his gaze on the same thing that had captured the full attention of his mother, brothers, and sisters—a gargantuan green dragon who was glaring down at him, growling angrily.

For a frozen moment, no one spoke. The young dragon could only stare, quaking with fright. Basilgarrad, for his part, was in no hurry. And Gwynnia, worried as she was about the safety of her child, didn't want to do anything that might antagonize this gigantic predator who could gobble up her whole family in the blink of an eye.

Finally, Basilgarrad turned to Gwynnia. As their gazes met, he said the last thing she ever expected: "Hello, sister. Remember me?"

Gwynnia gasped, and her triangular eyes opened to their widest. Deep in her orange pupils, a spark of recognition flared as she recalled that bizarre connection she'd felt with a tiny green lizard she'd met long before. A lizard who looked much like this dragon—except infinitely smaller.

"Y-y-you?" she stammered. "From Merlin's wedding? But you were—you were so . . . so very—"

"Small?"

Gwynnia nodded, making the iridescent purple scales on her neck flash like jewels.

"Yes. Small enough to be torn apart and eaten by one of your children." His ear flicked toward the quaking youth. "*That* one. Who, now that I'm fully grown, could make a tasty little morsel for my dessert."

"No, please," Gwynnia pleaded. "You won't eat my little Ganta, will you? He—well, he . . . didn't know any better."

"Then," declared the great green dragon, "it's time he learned."

Gwynnia, fearing the worst, gasped again. Several of her children whimpered; one dived under her wing.

Slowly, the massive head turned back to young Ganta. Peering into the small orange eyes, the gigantic dragon said, "I am Basilgarrad, defender of Avalon. And I have something to teach you."

Despite his quivering frame, the smaller dragon tried to hold his head high. "Punish me, master Basil . . . whatever. Do what you like. But please don't hurt my mother or my family."

The corner of Basilgarrad's mouth lifted ever so slightly. *I like that spirit. Maybe there's hope for this little fellow yet.*

"Well, Ganta, what do you think I'm going to do to you?"

"Anything you want, master Basil."

"And why is that?"

The little dragon's snout crinkled in surprise at being asked such an obvious question. "Because you're bigger, of course! If you're bigger, you do what you want."

Basilgarrad brought his face right up to the young dragon's. "No," he declared. "That's not right."

Ganta blinked, clearly puzzled.

"Bigness," said Basilgarrad, "is not about what you weigh. It's about what you *do*. How you act. How you treat others."

Pulling his face away, he continued, "Which is why, young Ganta, I'm not going to eat you." To keep the little fellow's attention, he added, "Not now, anyway."

Gwynnia joined her son in heaving a sigh.

Basilgarrad gave his sister a broad wink. "Besides, I really don't think he'd taste very good."

With that, he leaped skyward, pumping his mighty wings. He felt well fed, and also well entertained—but now he had serious work to do in the remote reaches of Waterroot. As he veered south, toward the lair of the water dragons, Gwynnia and her children watched with both awe and relief. And in the case of one young dragon . . . with intrigue.

14: BLUE ICE

What makes people so eager to fight me? I guess they don't put much value on my life. Or on theirs.

A colossal splash exploded, sending jets of water soaring skyward. For leagues around, fish and water birds and mer folk scattered, trying to escape whatever had hit the sea with such force. Even kelp and floating scraps of driftwood, pushed aside by the powerful waves, seemed to swim away.

Basilgarrad had arrived in the Rainbow Seas.

He scanned the ocean around him, laced with iridescent streaks of color, then drew a deep breath of the briny air. Paddling with his wings, as if they were enormous flippers, and using his immense tail as a rudder, he turned himself around to face the rugged coastline. Following the line of sheer cliffs, he saw, directly ahead, the mouth of a huge cave. Colorful shells ringed the entrance, barnacles by the thousands clung to the rocks, and the air smelled of fish and otters and seals.

Basilgarrad peered at the gaping mouth of the cave, hoping this was the place he'd been seeking. Yet his thoughts were heavy with doubt. *This isn't what I expected.*

He frowned, knowing that time was short. He couldn't

afford to spend days and days searching for Bendegeit's lair. The blight was spreading—and whatever was causing it, and Avalon's other troubles, was surely growing stronger.

All at once, ocean spray shot upward right in front of him. Three great heads rose out of the waves—heads with massive, teeth-studded jaws, deep blue eyes, and finlike ears. The heads of water dragons. As the trio lifted higher, water cascaded off their ears and snouts, pouring over scales the color of glacial blue ice.

The dragons drew themselves together, linking their powerful shoulders. Barring the way to the cave entrance, they looked like an impassable wall that had suddenly jutted out of the sea. A wall with countless blue-tinted teeth.

"Come no closer," bellowed the dragon in the middle, who was somewhat larger than his companions. "Or you shall die."

Facing these fierce guardians of the cave, Basilgarrad said to himself, "Now *that's* what I expected."

Treading their flippers, the trio of water dragons advanced, holding their close formation. "Leave now," ordered the middle dragon, whose face bore a deep scar across his snout.

"I come in peace," declared Basilgarrad, still watching them carefully. "I must speak with your highlord Bendegeit."

"No one speaks with the highlord unless he so commands. Now leave."

"But I—"

The middle dragon tossed his head impatiently, spraying his

companions. The scar on his snout turned bright silver, the color of dragons' blood. "Leave! I shall count to three. One."

"I told you, I mean no harm." Recalling Merlin's firm admonition—avoid any battles—he repeated, "I come in peace."

The guardians advanced. "Two."

"Honestly, I—"

"Three. Charge!"

At the dragon's command, all three guardians swam forward, moving with astounding speed. Jaws open, eyes ablaze, they shot toward the intruder who dared to refuse to leave.

Basilgarrad, however, moved faster. Pulling his wings—which were much longer than the flippers that water dragons normally encountered—out of the sea, as fast as a pair of whips, he smashed the heads of the two outside dragons. Their skulls struck both sides of the middle dragon's, making a loud *crrunnnch*. As water sprayed all around, the two outside dragons teetered and fell over sideways, knocked unconscious.

The scarred dragon, stronger than the others (or just thicker in the skull), managed to stay upright. Though dazed, he roared wrathfully and started to attack, blowing a torrent of blue ice from his nostrils. Calmly, Basilgarrad solved this problem with a flick of his mighty tail. When the massive knob landed another blow on the water dragon's head, he keeled over, joining his companions.

To make sure they didn't drown, Basilgarrad wrapped his

tail around their necks to lift their heads out of the water. He swam toward the cave entrance, towing them to shore as a larger boat might pull three smaller boats into harbor. Dumping them safely on the barnacle-covered rocks, he gazed at them thoughtfully.

"Well," he muttered, "so much for no battles."

Turning away from the unconscious guards, he sailed into the mouth of the cave. He did not notice, protruding from the waves a short way out to sea, the top of another dragon's head. Its eyes, a richer, luminous blue that glittered like water-washed azure, watched his movements closely. As he entered the cave, the hidden dragon followed.

To Basilgarrad's surprise, the cave didn't grow any darker as he sailed deeper. Quite the opposite: The farther he swam into the tunnel, the brighter it became. Then, all at once, it expanded into a vast, high-ceilinged cavern bathed in pearly light. The source of that light was an array of torches suspended from the rock walls. But these torches differed from any he'd ever seen. Instead of bearing flames, they held clear bubbles of seaglass filled with phosphorescent water from the ocean depths.

Lit by the gleaming torches, the cavern's walls arched high overhead. Iridescent paua shells, shimmering with violet and blue, lined all the lower surfaces. On the shells' protruding edges sat dozens of loons, terns, egrets, and flying crabs—all cooing, whistling, and snapping. On the ceiling, sea stars of gold, blue, green, and red had been arranged into a mosaic of many scenes: dragons sailing bravely out to sea, water birds wheeling through misty skies, nets of woven kelp hauling loads of fish, and an enormous dragon wearing a crown studded with undersea coral and jewels.

Bendegeit, thought the green dragon as he swam toward the center of the cavern. His nostrils flared. Mixed with the dominant smells of water birds, algae, sea salt, kelp, and barnacles, he detected one more smell. Elusive but unmistakable, the smell seemed as rich and deep as the sea itself.

He nodded grimly. It was the smell of dragons—one dragon in particular. A dragon who had made this cavern, like this undersea realm, his own domain.

The water before him began to roil, churning with conflicting currents. All at once, a huge head rose out of the surface, rivers of water pouring off its immense snout and brow. A crown of golden coral, studded with diamond and emeralds, topped the head. More jewels, mostly rubies, had been set within barnacles that lined the toothy jaws. But none of these jewels glowed as bright as this dragon's eyes. Unlike the azure blue eyes of the dragon who had followed Basilgarrad—and who continued to watch him closely from the far side of the cavern—this dragon's eyes glowed orange with flecks of scarlet, as if they were aflame.

"You darrrrre to enterrrrr my caverrrrrn?" he rumbled. "The lairrrrr of Bendegeit, highlorrrrrd of the waterrrrr drrrrrragons?"

"I do," answered Basilgarrad, holding his own head high.

Although he was even bigger than the highlord, it wasn't by much; never before had he met another dragon so close to his own size. "But I come in peace, at the request of Merlin."

"You know the wizarrrrrd, then?" The water dragon's finlike ears, lined with blue scales, swiveled at the rim of his crown. "You must have used Merrrrrlin's magic to elude my guarrrrrds."

"Not exactly." Basilgarrad's tongue played with the gap between his front teeth. "They seemed . . . a bit tired. Especially Scarface. So I merely persuaded them to take a midday nap."

The fires of the highlord's eyes flared with new brightness—whether from anger or amusement, it was impossible to tell. "Tell me then, grrrrreat brrrrringerrrrr of naps, what is yourrrrr name and purrrrrpose? Then I shall decide yourrrrr fate."

At the far side of the cavern, the hidden head of the azure-eyed dragon rose a bit higher from the water. The head's ears tilted forward, listening.

"My name is Basilgarrad. And I have come, great highlord, to ask you for help. Troubles are now spreading across Avalon! Is someone behind all this? Who? We need to know that, and soon!"

He brought his face closer to the highlord's so their jaws almost touched. "I ask for your help, your power of Undersight—not for my sake, or Merlin's. I ask this for Avalon."

The great water dragon growled deep in his throat, making Basilgarrad pull back. Then Bendegeit's nostrils flared. Two jets of glacial blue ice shot out from them and smacked into the water, forming a pair of small icebergs. The icebergs tilted on the waves, nearly capsizing, then started to float toward the nearest wall of the cavern.

"You have wasted yourrrrr time coming herrrrre," boomed the highlord. "And much worrrrrse, you have wasted mine! I am the unrrrrrivalled masterrrrr of Waterrrrroot. Why should I carrrrre about the rrrrrest of Avalon, farrrrr beyond the borrrrrderrrrrs of my rrrrrealm?"

The green eyes of Basilgarrad flashed. "Because," he declared, his voice resounding on the cavern walls, "what happens in one part of Avalon affects the other parts as well! If the tail of a fish is wounded, can that fish still swim and leap? If the wing of a bird is maimed, can that bird still soar and dive? This evil may not have reached you yet but if it isn't stopped, it surely will."

"We speak not of fish and birrrrrds! We speak of my rrrrrealm." Bendegeit's teeth, streaked with green algae, glinted in the light of the torches. "Now, grrrrrreen visitorrrrrr, you must deparrrrrt—beforrrrrre I summon the rrrrrest of my guarrrrrds."

"But highl—"

"Deparrrrrt!" The water dragon roared so loud that dozens of sea stars, clinging to the ceiling mosaic, broke loose and splashed into the water.

As the echoes faded, the two dragons glared at each other, one unwilling to leave and the other unwilling to change his mind. Again Bendegeit growled, deeper than before, as daggerlike shards of ice sprayed from his nose. Now his fiery eyes seemed ready to explode.

Meanwhile, Basilgarrad's mind raced through his options—none of them appealing. If he fought the highlord, what would he gain? Even if he won, the water dragon could still refuse to help. And if he left, as Bendegeit commanded, what would all this have accomplished? How could he tell Merlin that he'd failed completely? His wings stirred uneasily in the water—for he sensed a battle was imminent.

The tension increased. Muscles tensed in both of the huge dragons' necks, backs, and tails. The highlord's sprays of ice grew stronger; Basilgarrad's tail lifted higher, until it almost broke the surface of the water.

Seconds passed. The cavern seemed to be filling with pressure, as if it were a bubble—a bubble about to burst.

"Wait." This new voice, higher and clearer than that of either of the two opposing dragons, rang out in the cavern.

Both Basilgarrad and Bendegeit, while keeping one eye on each other, turned toward the voice. At the far side of the cavern, another head was swiftly rising out of the water. Though its features were more delicate, the head was almost as large as the highlord's. And it eyes, luminous azure blue, burned with a light as strong as any dragon's. Water flowed from sparkling blue scales, until the entire head and neck had lifted into the air.

"Marrrrrnya," said the highlord with a rumbling growl, "you should not be herrrrre!"

"Yes, I should, Father," she replied crisply. "For I must speak to you."

"Now, daughterrrrr?"

"Now."

Smoothly, hardly making any ripples, Marnya approached. Focusing her azure blue gaze upon her father, she beseeched him, "Please, my lord, I ask you a boon. Just one."

Bendegeit's brow creased, tilting his crown forward. "What boon does my daughterrrrr desirrrrrre?"

In the seconds before she answered, Basilgarrad wondered the same thing. What could she possibly want? The head of this green intruder on a stake? The chance to deal the death blow herself?

"I heard your conversation with this dragon." She waved a flipper at Basilgarrad, spraying him with seawater. "And I want you to grant his request."

Bendegeit started in surprise—as did the green dragon opposite him. "Why, my daughterrrrr, would you ask such a thing? What does this wrrrrretched intrrrrruderrrrr mean to you?"

Slowly, she turned her azure eyes on Basilgarrad. "He," she announced with certainty, "is the dragon I've been waiting for. The one who will teach me how to fly."

15: SPIRALS

Many are the ways to soar—some more thrilling, and more deadly, than others.

Fly?" asked Bendegeit and Basilgarrad in unison. Their deep voices boomed like simultaneous thunderclaps, echoing around the torchlit cavern, knocking off several more sea stars from the ceiling.

Keeping her luminous blue eyes fixed on Basilgarrad, Marnya nodded decisively.

"My daughterrrrr, you must—" began the highlord. But he stopped himself, considering a new idea. With a wry grin, he reached out of the water with one of his flippers and straightened his bejeweled crown, then declared, "Yourrrrr rrrrrequest shall be grrrrranted. If the intrrrrruderrrrr herrrrre can teach you to fly, then I will show him the trrrrrrue cause of his trrrrrroubles."

"How—but, I . . . but . . ." sputtered the green dragon, caught entirely by surprise. Looking from Marnya to her father and back again, he finally managed to say, "But I don't know how! She's—you're—a *water* dragon."

"Nonetheless," rumbled Bendegeit with a smirk on his titanic lips, "that is my decrrrrree. Accept my condition—orrrrr leave this rrrrrealm rrrrright now."

Basilgarrad, boiling over with frustration at this turn of events, shook his head. Time was wasting! Yet he had no choice.

"I accept," he growled. Turning to the young female dragon, he added, "We start now. This minute."

"Excellent," she replied, beaming. "I have always wanted to fly. Always! But no one here can teach me. When I saw you land, I knew that you were the one to do it."

"How perrrrrfect," said the highlord, his eyes burning brightly. "This will be rrrrratherrrrr amusing."

"Right," grumbled Basilgarrad. "Follow me." Shaking his head, he spun himself around and started to swim back down the tunnel to the open sea. Close behind followed the highlord and his daughter.

As he passed beyond the pearly light of the cavern, Basilgarrad's mind churned with troublesome questions. How could he possibly teach her to fly if she didn't even have wings? Just how had that slippery eel of a highlord gotten the better of him? Was there still some way to get Bendegeit's help?

As soon as they emerged from the tunnel, Marnya's flying lessons began in earnest. They did not go well. With the amused highlord and his three unconscious guards (still slumped together on the rocky shore) as an audience, Basilgarrad tried to show her how to take flight, launching from the water. He pushed her from behind while she flapped madly, pulled her with his tail, and did everything he could think of to encourage her. But nothing worked. She could no sooner lift herself out of the water than she could magically transform her flippers into feathered wings.

At one point, a flock of seabirds—silver kingfishers—flew overhead. So close to the water they came, the dragons paused to watch them float above the waves, their wide wings reflecting the rich colors of the sea. Basilgarrad listened to the wings' rhythmic swishing, drew a deep breath of salty air, and shook his head sadly.

Marnya, too, felt discouraged. As she watched the birds fly past so effortlessly, her eyes lost some of their radiance. And the highlord of the water dragons? His face, unlike the others, showed glowing satisfaction.

"Arrrrre you rrrrready to give up, Marrrrrnya?" Bendegeit called to his daughter.

"Not nearly, Father!" she replied. But the forced tone of her voice belied her words.

Basilgarrad, at that moment, decided to try a different approach, focusing on how to move her flippers. "It's different than moving through water," he explained, holding her flipper just above the surface. "Air, like water, is strong enough to support our weight. But it's different—lighter, thinner. To fly, you can't just row through it. You first need to *place* yourself on it, then *glide* upon it."

"How can I glide on the air," she asked in exasperation, "if I can't even get out of the water?"

"By using your flippers more like wings!" he said for what seemed like the hundredth time.

"I don't know what that means!" she protested. "Isn't there any way you can show me?"

"That's what I've been trying to do all this time!" he said crossly.

"Well, it isn't working. Can't you show me more clearly?"

"Not unless I—" He caught himself. "Wait! I have an idea. It might not work. But if it does . . . it just might show you what you need to see. And, Marnya"—he glanced over at Bendegeit, impatiently blowing streams of ice out of his nose—"we're running out of time."

"I know," she replied. "Whatever this idea is, let's try it."

"All right. You need to trust me. Do you?"

She peered at him for a long moment, her blue eyes sparkling like ocean mist. "Yes."

"Then stay right where you are while I dive beneath you and . . ."

"Lift me into the air?" Her azure eyes opened wide. "You can do that?"

"I can try! Because the only way to show you how wings really move is to let you see up close what I do when I fly. Then, perhaps, you can do it yourself." He frowned. "I'm just not sure I can lift someone as big as you."

"Try!" she pleaded, splashing the water with her fins. "This really could work!" Lowering her voice, she added,

"Don't forget, you're not doing this for me. You're doing it for Avalon."

Her words gave him a new burst of energy, as a spark ignites kindling. Without waiting another instant, he swam some distance behind her, filled his lungs with the briny air, and dived under the waves.

Whooooosh! He rose out of the waves just beneath her, working his tail furiously to gain forward momentum. With a mighty heave, he lifted her onto his back—but could he possibly carry her into the air? Stretching his huge wings to the fullest, he worked them with all his strength, straining to lift this heavy load above the surface of the sea. Never had he thrown so much effort into beating, beating, beating his wings!

Marnya, meanwhile, held on to his back, wrapping her claws around his muscular shoulders. All the while, she watched the powerful sweep of his wings, trying to understand how they caught the air—enough to glide.

Smashing through the water, shooting spray in all directions, Basilgarrad threw every bit of his strength into trying to take off. He whipped his wings, waved his tail, and stretched his neck upward. Harder he tried, and harder, ignoring the weight that pressed him down and the growing aches in his back, shoulders, and tail.

Lift her, Basil! he commanded. *Lift her!*

Finally . . .

He rose out of the water. Rising skyward, he climbed slowly, bit by bit, until his wingtips and tail no longer splashed against the surface. At last, completely airborne, he beat his wings powerfully, carrying his passenger higher. Soon they were soaring far above the water—and the highlord who sat watching them in amazement.

"You did it!" trumpeted Marnya.

"Yes," he replied, a ring of satisfaction in his voice. "Now watch carefully."

Arching his wings backward, he suddenly stalled in mid-air. Even as his passenger gasped in fright, he changed the wings' angle, catching an updraft that carried them higher. Then, banking to the side, he spun several tight turns, spiraling around and around far above the iridescent sea.

"This is marvelous," she said dreamily, speaking right into his ear. "If only I could—no! Wait!"

Relaxing for an instant, she had allowed a claw to slip off his shoulder. Pulled by the force of his spiraling turns, she started to lose her grip. Her balance. And her only support.

"Help!" she screamed, sliding completely off his back.

Basilgarrad rolled underneath her, trying to give her new purchase. But she couldn't grab hold in time. Her claws scraped down the scales of his back—then touched only air.

"Help me!" she cried, tumbling downward.

Basilgarrad stopped spiraling, veered, then plunged after her as fast as he could. But he knew, given the distance between them, that he could never reach her in time. The same realization had also struck her father, far below, who was bellowing and waving his flippers wildly.

Marnya, spinning as she dropped, could see the blue expanse of the sea approaching at an alarming rate. Though she'd never experienced anything like this before, she sensed that hitting the water at this speed would be almost as violent as hitting solid land. She might or might not live, but could easily break her flippers, her back, or her neck.

Her mind raced. What do birds do to slow down? How do they turn a fall into a flight?

Instinctively, she arched her back, trying to lift her head so it wouldn't be the first part of her to hit the water. At the same time, she stretched out her flippers—long and sturdy, if narrower than wings—more from the natural urge to grab hold of something than to accomplish any real goal. As her head lifted, she found her belly taking more of the wind. And with her body more horizontal, her flippers, too, caught more air. The webbing along the flippers' edges expanded, opening to the rushing wind.

Gradually, her headlong plunge became more of a diagonal descent. Holding her flippers out wide, she slowed herself slightly, feeling the substance of the air beneath her body. She tilted her flippers to the rear, slowing some more and gaining a tiny bit of control. Angling her belly upward, she could almost feel supported by the invisible blanket beneath her.

In seconds, she had changed from an object plummeting *through* the air . . . to a creature riding *on* the air. Now she was drifting. Gliding.

Flying!

Flippers outstretched, she slid into the sea, spraying a

huge wave of water that drenched her father. But he didn't seem to mind. As he swam over to greet her, nearly losing his crown in all his excitement, she turned her gaze skyward.

Thank you, green dragon, she thought as she watched him descend. *For this gift. This flight.*

16: SHADOWS

What we see is useful, provocative, or inspiring. But what we don't see is essential.

True to his promise, the regal Bendegeit, having satisfied himself that Marnya hadn't suffered any broken bones, agreed to help Basilgarrad. He spun around on the glittering waves, splashing water in all directions, and started to lead his beaming daughter and their now-honored guest back to his hidden cavern. There, where his magic was strongest, he would grant the boon.

As they neared the mouth of the cave, the three unconscious guardian dragons, sprawled on the rocks, began to stir. Just as Basilgarrad sailed by, the dragon with the scarred snout awoke fully—and gaped. Seeing the dastardly intruder who had bested him was upsetting enough, but to see that intruder swimming contentedly alongside the highlord and his daughter was more than the guardian could bear. He roared wrathfully at Basilgarrad and lunged at his foe, spraying blue icicles on the rocks.

Alas, he failed to notice that his tail had been tied into a knot with the tails of his companions—a small precaution that

Basilgarrad had taken before leaving them. As a result, the lunging water dragon suddenly came to a halt and hurtled backward. He smashed, with more angry roars, right on top of his companions. All three guardians fell to kicking and biting each other, only tangling themselves more.

"Ahoy there, Scarface!" called Basilgarrad as he sailed past. "Have a nice nap?"

No answer came but for a chorus of growls, roars, and bashing heads.

Moments later, the highlord and his daughter plus Basilgarrad reached the luminous cavern. Torches, holding the phosphorescent light of the sea, projected the three dragons' shadows against the walls. The green, blue, and purple paua shells glowed even more radiantly than Basilgarrad remembered. He shook himself with anticipation, knowing he would soon learn the answer to his—and Avalon's—biggest question.

Glancing up at the high ceiling with its colorful mosaics made of sea stars, he said to the highlord, "Something tells me that a new mosaic might be added sometime soon."

"And what prrrrompts you to say that?"

"Just a guess," said the green dragon mirthfully. "A historical scene would be nice—say, the first water dragon ever to fly."

Bendegeit's eyes gleamed with amusement. "Perrrrrhaps you arrrrre rrrrright."

Marnya chortled gleefully. She turned her azure gaze on Basilgarrad, watching him with gratitude.

Floating in the center of the cavern, the highlord of the water dragons cleared his throat, a deep rumbling that echoed around the walls. His expression now serious, he faced Basilgarrad and commanded, "State the question you wish me to answerrrrr."

The green dragon's eyebrows lifted. "What—or who—is behind Avalon's troubles? The fighting, the fraying peace, the spreading blight. Who is causing this?"

Bendegeit inhaled a deep breath, as if he were breathing in the very question. Then, with a powerful slap of his flipper, he struck the water's surface, sending a great fountain of spray into the air. Countless droplets, sparkling in the torches' light, rose toward the ceiling, slowed their ascent, then hovered for an instant before raining downward.

All but one droplet.

For Bendegeit had chosen that particular droplet for his purpose. Training his gaze on its silvery round shape, he called on his inner magic to hold it in place, high above their heads. Like a solitary star it gleamed—unique, lovely, and alone.

The highlord's orange eyes narrowed as he concentrated on the droplet. Slowly, very slowly, it started to expand, swelling into a silvery sphere that twirled brightly before them. The sphere reflected the light of the torches, as well as the brilliant colors of the shells and sea stars on the cavern walls. Yet it also radiated a different kind of light—a subtle, shifting light of its own.

"Hearrrrrken now, spherrrrre!" boomed Bendegeit. Then, his voice a whispery growl, he began to chant:

Write the unwritten,
Find what is lost,
Tell the untold.
Scry the forgotten,
Suffer the cost—
Open the fold.

Show what lies hidden,
Dark to the eye,
Wondrous or bleak.
Share now unbidden,
The ultimate why—
Truth do I seek.

Light and shadow began to whirl within the sphere, spinning and shimmering. For an instant, the globe brightened, as radiant as an exploding star. Then, inexorably, the light dimmed. Shadows darkened, blackness deepened, coalescing in edges and shapes that seemed devoid of light.

Darker than dark was the phrase that leaped into Basilgarrad's mind. Without knowing why, he shuddered.

A figure appeared in the center of the sphere, blacker than the shadows that surrounded it. Long and sinewy, like a vertical snake, it seemed to be laboring somehow—not drinking, not eating, not working with tools. What could it be doing? Something requiring great strength and concentration. Perhaps . . . giving birth?

Something about the figure's shape felt vaguely familiar to

Basilgarrad. Yet he couldn't begin to explain why. Because at this moment the shadow leech was not showing its bloodred eye, its identity remained concealed. Though Basilgarrad stared hard into the shimmering sphere, he could only be sure that his hunch was correct: All of Avalon's recent troubles *did* have a single source, an identifiable cause. But exactly what that cause was, and where in Avalon it might be found, he did not know.

The dark image in the sphere started to fade, blurring into layers of shadows. Just as the image vanished completely, the sphere itself began to shrink, condensing down into the size of a single drop of water.

The highlord nodded, his jewel-studded visage grim. "Do you rrrrrecognize that wicked crrrrreaturrrrre?" he asked Basilgarrad.

Merlin's great friend shook his head sadly.

"So tell me . . . do you underrrrrstand anything morrrrre now than you did beforrrrrre?"

"Only this, highlord." Basilgarrad's voice rumbled so loud the cavern vibrated. "Somewhere, that creature is working evil—enough to threaten our whole world. I don't know its plans, its powers, or even its name. But I do know one thing."

"What is that?" asked Marnya, swimming closer.

Basilgarrad lifted his head high, stretching up nearly to the cavern's ceiling. Light from the phosphorescent torches glinted on his scales and teeth. "Somehow I'm going to find that shadowy thing. Find it—and destroy it."

"But we have the solution!" cried Lleu triumphantly. He practically bounced to his feet beside her. Straightening his frayed brown tunic, the simple garb of a priest, he added, "Your brother has the crystal of pure élano, remember? The blight is as good as ended."

"Not so, Lleu." The wizard's voice, still weary from the strain of obtaining the crystal, sounded heavy with doubt. "I have the crystal, yes. But it will do no good if we can't set it in the right place."

The others' heads turned toward Merlin. Slowly, legs wobbling, he stood. Leaning heavily against his staff, he surveyed the desolate scene around them. Except for the flickering green flames between the stone pillars, there was no movement, no sign of life. For as far as he could see, the landscape consisted of skeletal trees devoid of leaves, empty gullies without a trickle of water, and ashen soil.

"What do you mean, the right place?" asked Rhia as she, too, clambered to her feet. Her suit of woven vines, now almost completely brown, crackled as she stood. Leaves, brittle and dry, crumbled and fell to the ground by her bare feet.

Merlin swung around to face her. Twisting the tip of his staff into the lifeless soil, he said grimly, "The blight has expanded, both in size and power, since we left. Just look around us—so much devastation."

Wearily, he sighed. "For the crystal to work, I'm convinced we need to place it precisely in the center of the blight. I don't mean the physical center, but the *magical* center. The place where the blight really began, its true origin. That's the only place where this dark magic can be fully stopped. And that's far from here, very far."

"How do you know that?" his sister demanded.

"I can feel it." He put one hand upon his chest. "Right here."

"Well," suggested Lleu, stepping closer, "can't we just go there? To a portal that's closer to the center?" He glanced at the fire, weakly sputtering between the pillars. "This isn't the same one we entered, the one that took us to the white lake. If we just ride back to that one, we could—"

"I refuse," grumbled Nuic, his little hands balled into fists.

"Even if we tried," said Merlin, "I doubt it would work. These portals around Woodroot are all suffering from the same dark magic, whatever its source, that's afflicted the land. We barely made it here as it was! I wouldn't want to enter another portal until they are restored to power—or else we might never come out again."

"For once," Nuic muttered, "you're talking sensibly."

Rhia studied her brother. "What about your power of Leaping? Could you send yourself there, with the crystal?"

Slowly, he shook his head, sweeping his black hair across his shoulders. "No, Rhia. I can barely stand, let alone Leap! That whole experience at the lake . . . I'm so drained, there isn't a chance."

Reaching into his pocket, he pulled out the crystal. Its seven facets, gleaming radiantly, shone like pure light in his hand. Closing his fingers around it, he muttered, "There must be a way. There must."

He caught his breath. "There *is* one way! That is, if Basil didn't run into trouble."

Knowing what had occurred to him, Rhia nodded. "Call him! We can ride him to the center of the blight."

Shuffling across the dusty ground, Nuic's color darkened. "Maybe we should try the portal after all. Riding that clumsy serpent is like riding a nightmare."

"Hush," said Rhia, lifting the sprite. "He's our best chance."

"Then we're as good as dead," he grumbled, settling into the bend of her arm.

Merlin raised his eyes skyward. His bushy brows drew together; concentration creased his brow. "Basil, old boy . . ." he said pleadingly. "Are you anywhere near Woodroot? If so . . . I could use a ride. Sometime soon. *Very* soon."

"How about right now?" boomed a thunderous voice that rolled out of the southern sky.

As the group wheeled around, a shadow appeared in a high, spiraling cloud of dust. The shadow solidified, then out of the cloud burst Basilgarrad, Avalon's mightiest dragon. His enormous wings seemed like twin islands floating on the air, though no island could bend and twist with such grace and flexibility. He banked a turn, the scales on his chest glistening green. Arching his back and tail, he coasted to a landing on the ground beside Merlin and the others.

"Hmmmpff," growled Nuic. "What took you so long?"

Basilgarrad, seeing the look of urgency on Merlin's face, didn't answer. Within seconds, the group had climbed aboard his massive brow and were flying swiftly northward. Merlin, holding tight to one of the dragon's ears, scanned the lifeless landscape below, as the wind swept past. Searching both outward and inward, he seemed to be wrapped in a shroud of deep concentration.

"There!" he cried at last. "That's the spot."

He pointed ahead, at a round, gray patch of land. Not even a skeletal tree or a leafless shrub grew there. The soil looked even more drained than what they had seen elsewhere—totally sapped of nutrients, like a bloodless corpse. A stale, putrid smell wafted toward them, making Basilgarrad scowl.

Nevertheless, he landed in the middle of the deathly patch. Clouds of dust rose all around them as he touched down, clogging the putrid air. Yet no one, not even the sprite, complained. The stakes were too high. Almost before Basilgarrad came to a stop, the wizard started to climb down.

Merlin walked over to an especially ashen spot. His face haggard, he looked much older than his years; like Rhia's brittle suit of vines, he suffered along with this once-bountiful realm. Carefully, he pulled the luminous crystal from his tunic.

Supported by his staff, he kneeled down and placed the crystal on the ground. Peering into its radiant facets, he said quietly, "Bring life back to this land . . . I beg of you."

Slowly, the wizard stood. He glanced uncertainly at Rhia, then at Basilgarrad. Anxiously, he twisted his staff into the dead ground. Seconds passed, seeming like hours. Nothing happened.

More time passed. Still nothing happened.

Basilgarrad's ears trembled. He thought he heard something—a distant chiming sound, like a faraway bell.

The sound swelled, growing stronger, until everyone else could hear its sonorous ring. Rhia caught her breath, realizing that the dead vines on her arm had started to bend and twirl, as if nudged by a gentle breeze. Only there was no breeze, at least not the physical sort that stirs the air. Rather, this was a stirring of the soul, an awakening of life.

All at once, the crystal began to vibrate. An explosion of light, both white and green, suddenly burst from its center—spreading outward in glowing circles that expanded like ripples on a pond. Farther the ripples spread, and farther, passing through the ground, reaching toward the horizon.

Meanwhile, the vines on Rhia's suit continued to move, turning toward the crystal, just as flowers turn toward the light. The vines grew more supple, even as hints of green appeared in their stems and leaves. Rhia's eyes danced, for she could feel their life returning. Even crusty old Nuic, resting in the crook of her arm, began to turn a subtle shade of green.

The bell's chiming grew stronger, ringing all around them, vibrating in the air. From the soil, meanwhile, a single green shoot pushed skyward, breaking out of the ground, reaching for freedom. Higher it rose, and still higher. More shoots sprouted nearby, then more, until the ground seemed to boil with greenery. Hundreds of plants, then thousands, pushed upward, twisting with vitality and celebrating new life.

Leaves in great abundance grew from the branches and twigs of once-dead trees. A new sound filled the air—the liquid rush of flowing water, rising from underground springs, splashing down rivulets. Now the wind stirred the boughs of the reviving forest, rustling the leaves and stroking the bushes and grasses. In time, all these sounds—of bells, of water, and of wind—merged into one melodious song.

"Alive," whispered Merlin, his voice hoarse but full of new energy. He turned toward the deepening vista of woodland stretching to the horizon on every side.

"Alive," echoed Rhia, running her hand over the living vines that embraced her arm.

For now, thought Basil, recalling the image of the writhing black shape he had seen in the water dragon's lair. Darker than dark it seemed—and, even now, amidst so much new life, it cast a shadow upon his heart.

So awash in thoughts was he that, like the others, he didn't notice the small black leech that crawled out of the ground near the crystal. Quivering with anguish, the leech managed to flash its bloodred eye only briefly, sending some sort of message before it died.

18: A Chilling Sound

Plans, like seedlings, need some sort of light to grow. Unless they are plans that thrive, instead, on darkness.

Deep in the Haunted Marsh, a sudden cry erupted. Screeching horribly, echoing among the rotting corpses of the pit, the cry reverberated in the foul night air. Every creature within earshot froze at the sound, quaking with terror that slid slowly through the marrow of their bones. Even creatures without bones, such as the marsh ghouls, trembled in fear.

The huge, swollen leech who had uttered that cry was, itself, quaking. But not with fright. No, that great beast, darker than all the shadows around it, quaked with rage. Absolute rage. Wrath oozed out of its every pore, sliding down its skin like poisonous perspiration.

Doomraga cried out again—with rage, as before, but also with something else. Something more like determination.

"That miserable green dragon and that wizard he carries," it uttered in a chilling whisper. "Meddlers. Troublemakers. We will destroy them, my master and I. Yes . . . just as we will destroy their world."

The monster's bloodred eye flashed, briefly illuminating

the marsh. For minutes thereafter, the rotting bodies and corrupt beings nearby glowed with a dull red hue. They pulsed, like dying stars, throbbing with the evil light.

Marshaling all its power, Doomraga returned to work. Its body started to bulge, expanding with rhythmic bursts of energy. Soon, the leech knew, it would achieve its most astonishing feat. Out of its new body would emerge a great new force, a most potent weapon, a power that would reach every corner of Avalon.

With that glimpse of the future, Doomraga quaked once more. This time, however, it did so not in rage . . . but in laughter. A deep, bone-rattling laugh arose from its core, echoing across the marsh.

19: THE MISTY PORTAL

Sometimes it's best not to know what lies ahead. Or even to guess.

Misty colors aglow, thousands and thousands of flowers trembled in the breeze. Intense purple, deep green, luminous pink—these and many other colors flashed brightly, covering ridges that rolled all the way to the horizon. Like most flowers in Airroot, they grew on the dense, compacted slopes of older clouds, where the airy soil was thick enough to support their roots. But here, in the oldest clouds of the realm, they had spread across misty meadows that rose and fell as far as anyone could see, making the clouds themselves gleam like crushed rainbows. No wonder, then, that bards had come to call this place the Cloud Gardens.

On one ridge in particular, where emerald green flowers painted the slope, color radiated. Here, green saturated the air above the flowers as well as the flowers themselves, glowing in the vapors that spiraled up from every blossom. And this radiant green seemed more than just color. Richer, brighter, it looked almost like a kind of flame. Green flame—rising out of the flowers, the mist, and the magical air.

The portal, shimmering with a strange sort of fire that was partly mist and partly light, was unique in all of Avalon. No other portal's flames matched these. And no one but the mist faeries and sylphs who lived near the Cloud Gardens, floating above the flowered ridges, knew it even existed. The misty portal remained a secret, undiscovered by outsiders and un-used by anyone.

Until now.

The vaporous fire crackled loudly, shooting green sparks that flamed bright before tumbling down to join the emerald flowers. There, with a watery hiss, the sparks melted away. The portal's fire, meanwhile, snapped and sparked more in-tensely than ever, like flames on a rolling boil.

The misty portal suddenly parted, opening into a deep green hole. Out of that hole reached a shape—a long, slender finger. Then came other fingers, knuckles, and the palm of a hand, emerging slowly. The hand groped, feeling the air outside the portal—as if testing to make sure the air really existed.

All at once, the hand lunged forward. Arm, shoulder, and head pushed through the curtain of mist, as a tall man stepped forward. He stood on the slope, luminous with flowers, looked around himself, and nodded.

"So," declared Krystallus, "there *is* a portal into Airroot." His rugged face creased in a grin. "How very disappointed Serella will be that I, not she, found it first."

He studied the shimmering portal, gazing at it as intently as a master jeweler would gaze at a new kind of crystal.

"Flames of mist," he said with wonder. "This is why I travel all the time—to find places like this."

He pushed off his brow a lock of hair, whiter than most clouds. And frowned, thinking of someone else—a man whose hair was as black as a raven's wing. For he knew there was another reason why he traveled constantly: to get away from his father. Not just the man, but his image, his reputation.

His *shadow*. A shadow that stretched from one end of this world to another, always touching Krystallus, always obscuring him. He squeezed his powerful hands into fists. Would he ever step out of that shadow? Or would he always be, as the elf queen Serella had said, just "the son of someone great"? Was his yearning to travel nothing more than a desire to escape?

Peering at the misty portal, he wondered what secrets it held. And what secrets he himself held. *Will I ever stop being Krystallus, son of Merlin—and become Krystallus Eopia, great explorer of Avalon?*

The fiery green curtain crackled, undulating as if beckoning to him. Could it lead higher in the Tree, to places no one had ever seen? To realms not yet discovered? To the uncharted stars?

His eyes reflecting the portal's green light, Krystallus knelt on the compacted cloud. Pulling his sketchbook out of his tunic pocket, he dipped his feather pen into the ink and began to draw a map. This one, different from any other map he'd drawn, showed masses of clouds, not land or water. Cloudscapes that rose, fell, merged, formed, and evaporated continuously, right before his eyes. This scene changed so rapidly, so fluidly, he found it necessary to sketch not one, but two, then three, then *seven* distinct versions—each one drawn a few minutes apart, each one showing a unique view of this realm of shifting mist.

Someday, he vowed, *I will create a new kind of map for this realm, a map that constantly evolves. Yes—just like these clouds!*

Quickly, he made a note of this idea (on the inside cover of the sketchbook, where he'd already scrawled many other ideas for new and better maps). Then, closing the book with a satisfying *snap,* he replaced it in his pocket.

And now, he thought, *where should I go next?* Impulsively, he picked seven petals from the emerald green flowers growing beside him. Placing their vaporous petals on his open hand, he considered them. *One for each root-realm. Which shall it be?*

Closing his eyes, he allowed the fingers of his free hand to roam across the petals. Finally, he picked one that felt just right—though he couldn't even begin to explain why. When he opened his eyes, he gasped in surprise.

Shadowroot! He hadn't expected that. The dark realm was the only one he'd never visited. No one he'd ever met, except Basilgarrad, had actually gone there and returned to talk about it. And Basil had ridden there on the wind. Why, there probably wasn't even a portal to Shadowroot! Even if he tried to go there by portalseeking, he could easily be taken to somewhere else entirely. Or worse: His disassembled body could never be restored again.

Grimly, he set his jaw. *I'm going to Shadowroot. If I can.*

Taking one last moment to gaze at the lush, misty meadows surrounding him, he pushed their radiant colors from his mind. His thoughts focused on one color only. The color of eternal night.

Krystallus then strode right into the portal's misty green curtain. Flames crackled, swallowing him greedily. With a burst of sparks, he disappeared.

20: FIRE IN THE SKY

Dragons live a long time. A very long time. But some things, deeper than memory, live longer.

Krystallus plunged forward, tumbling out of the fiery portal. He rolled on the hard ground, immediately smelling its strange aroma, much like crushed mint but more tart. Sitting up, he blinked his eyes. Beyond the ground illuminated by the flickering green flames, he saw nothing.

Nothing but blackness.

Dark sky, and even darker contours of hills, surrounded him. But for the portal behind him, there was no light anywhere. Not even the hint of a distant campfire. Or a home. Or life of any kind.

"Welcome to Shadowroot," he whispered to himself, drawing his knees closer to his chest as he sat on the mint-scented ground. There was a note of triumph in his voice, to be sure. But there was also something else—something more like fear.

For there was, indeed, life here. If he believed the stories of the museos—the translucent, tear-shaped creatures who sang wondrous, deeply sorrowful songs—the realm they had escaped from held unimaginable terrors. Whatever evil had forced the museos to flee Shadowroot years before still haunted them today, giving their songs an undertone of dread. And that evil, no doubt, still remained in this realm . . . somewhere beyond the portal's frail ring of light.

Maybe this is one time I'll wait until later to draw my map! It wouldn't show much, anyway. Unless, he mused, *I can invent a new sort of map that reveals what can't be seen.* Finding that an appealing notion, he grinned—and made a mental note to add it to his list.

Slowly, he stood. Peering into the dark surroundings, he tried to see anything recognizable. Anything alive. But all he could see were layers upon layers of darkness. *Realm of endless night,* he thought, quoting some bard who had written a ballad about the escape of the museos. How did it go? He remembered only a shred:

> *Utter darkness haunts their dreams,*
> *Fever from their flight.*
> *Evermore they hear the screams:*
> *Realm of endless night.*

Feeling something brush against his wrist, he started. In the wavering green light from the portal, he saw a tiny, triangular stain on his skin. Black as the realm around him. Suddenly frightened, he shook his arm, trying to shake off the stain—and whatever wickedness it carried.

To his surprise, the black mark lifted off his wrist and fluttered in the air. Erratically, it flew past his face before disappearing into the darkness. A moth! He watched it vanish—then caught, once again, that scent of crushed mint.

Bringing his wrist up to his nose, he sniffed. Mint flooded his nostrils—tart but also remarkably sweet. He grinned at his discovery—as well as his foolishness. *So this realm, full of all that darkness and danger, also holds a fragrant little moth.*

Curious to explore more of Shadowroot, he glanced over his shoulder at the flaming portal. The gateway that clearly he, Krystallus Eopia, was the first person to discover. And the first person to pass through unharmed. Another victory over that gloating Serella! Then, peering straight ahead, he stepped across the hard ground, to the very edge of the portal's light.

Dark hills, barely distinguished from the lightless sky, stretched farther than he could see. So dark was this vista that he couldn't even tell what was in the foreground and what lay far beyond. Everything merged into a thick soup of night. A soup that would, no doubt, hold more than its share of unusual spices . . . and deadly poisons.

Yet unlike a moment earlier, this scene didn't make his heart race with fear. "Somewhere out there," he said quietly, "is a tiny, mint-scented moth."

Suddenly the sky changed. Arrows of fire, orange and gold, streaked high overhead, ripping the veil of darkness. Lightning? Falling stars? Krystallus caught his breath, gazing in awe at the fiery arcs.

No! he realized. *That's not lightning. It's—*

He paused, mind racing, trying to remember the words his mother had used to describe the creature who had come to his parents' wedding. A creature who resembled a man, with enormous wings—wings that burned with bright orange flames.

Fire angels.

He watched, spellbound, as the flaming people soared overhead, leaving trails of glowing orange in the sky. Dozens of fire angels flew high above, lighting this otherwise darkened realm. *Where are they going?* he wondered. *And why are they here?*

Finally, as the last of the luminous creatures flew past, Krystallus lowered his gaze to see what this momentary burst of light could reveal about the lands around him. He saw, more clearly now, the rugged hills that surrounded this spot. They rose into mountains that seemed to pierce the sky. *Evernight Peaks*, he said to himself, already choosing the name he'd add to his map of this realm.

Below the hills, a dark lake rested, its surface as still as a mirror. Even with the streaks of orange flame reflected in its water, the lake seemed like a pool of liquid darkness. Under the surface moved ominous, shadowy shapes that were still darker. *Lake of Shadows*, thought Krystallus.

Just as the last orange light faded from the sky, he saw something else—something he'd entirely missed before. Bodies! Bodies of—could it be?—elves!

Sprawled only a few paces away from the portal's ring of light, the elves lay motionless on the ground. They were twisted, as if still writhing, their final agony etched on their faces. Several of them had died with their arms stretched toward the portal. Groping for a chance to escape? From what?

Heedless of the encroaching darkness, Krystallus ran over to them. There were five, six, seven in all—and all of them were clearly dead. He clenched his jaw, partly out of sympathy for their terrible deaths from an unknown cause. And partly, he admitted to himself, out of disappointment that others had found this portal first.

In the final glow of light from the fire angels, he sensed a small movement. One of the elves—a woman with silvery blond hair—stirred ever so slightly. Her fingers clawed at the air, as her throat emitted a weak, dying gasp.

Krystallus stared at her, even as her form faded into darkness. For he knew that elf, knew her hair and her voice and her arrogant ways, which had often tormented his dreams.

"Serella," he growled. Jealousy and resentment filled his heart, as relentlessly as the returning night filled the landscape.

Yet . . . down inside, in his innermost self, he felt a different emotion. One he never would have expected to feel, certainly not for Serella. Sympathy. Not for her as a fellow explorer, but on a deeper level, as a fellow living being.

Hesitating no longer, he rushed to her side. Tripping on one of the other darkened bodies, he barely kept his balance, reaching her just as total darkness descended. He kneeled down, placed his hand upon her back, and felt the barest quiver of a breath. Then, sliding his arms underneath her, he stood, lifting her limp body.

Staggering toward the portal's flames, Krystallus forced himself to concentrate on his next destination—Waterroot, the home of Serella's people. If he could just get her back to her realm, where elven healers could tend to her, she might yet survive. *Waterroot*, he thought, conjuring memories of its iridescent waves, cool currents, and salty air.

Yet even as he crossed into the ring of green light, he couldn't entirely push from his thoughts the strange place he was leaving. Or, hefting the body in his arms, the strange prize he was taking with him.

21: STRANGE THOUGHTS

After all these years, the only thing I know for certain is that I don't know anything for certain.

Staggering out of the portal, Krystallus didn't even notice the crisp breeze that struck his face, let alone the sharp, briny smell of seawater. Exhausted from his journey, he kneeled on the wet, barnacle-covered rocks that surrounded the portal and carefully set down Serella's body. Waves from the sea sloshed against the shore only a few paces away, spraying her boots and leggings.

Completely lifeless, she seemed, her face a sickly gray color and her eyes still open but unseeing. Some sort of black, shadowy lines creased the skin of her neck and brow. Gazing down at her, Krystallus noticed for the first time the deep forest green color of her eyes.

Placing a hand on her torn blue tunic, just below her neck, he felt for any breathing. Not a trace. He leaned over her face, trying to feel even a slight rush of air from her nose or mouth. Again—nothing. When he placed a hand on the side of her neck, checking for a pulse, he did no better.

Serella showed no sign of life. She lay motionless on the

rocks, her silvery blond hair arrayed around her head like rays of light.

To his own surprise, Krystallus felt a sharp pang of disappointment. *Probably because I worked so hard to get her here*, he surmised. *Should have left her where I found her.*

He had, indeed, worked hard to keep her essence tied to his own throughout the journey. It felt sometimes that the portal's fires wanted to rip her away, to carry her off to some other destination. Or to swallow her life energy and merge it forever with that of the Great Tree. At such moments, Krystallus had fought hard to keep her with him—harder than he could now explain, given that she was not someone he cared for. She was, after all, his bitter enemy, someone who had never missed a chance to humiliate him.

Yet now, as he looked down on her face, serene even with the marks of death, he couldn't quite feel his old resentment toward her. She had clearly suffered in dying from whatever had attacked her in Shadowroot. And she had, in fact, been a worthy competitor. A foe, yes, but not really wicked. She was just . . .

A seagull glided above them, screeching, as he searched for the right word.

Better. He gulped, realizing the truth. *She was always better at exploring than me.* Serella had been the first to find Brynchilla, first to make contact with the flamelons—and now the first to face the perils of Shadowroot. *She always had the heart of an explorer.*

So she wasn't his enemy, after all. Or even merely a competitor. She was really something more, something he couldn't quite name.

Sadly, he reached for her neck again. Maybe he'd feel a trace of a pulse this time? Just as his hand touched the soft skin of her throat—

"Get him!"

Hearing the gruff voice, Krystallus turned around—just in time to see three elves running up the rocky beach, about to pounce on him. Even as he started to stand, they drew their long knives and spears. And their angry, wild-eyed faces made their intentions perfectly clear.

"Stop him!" cried one elf. "Before he escapes into that portal."

"Tried to strangle her, he did."

"You killed our queen!"

Krystallus barely gained his footing when another elf dashed out from behind the portal and leaped onto his back. Collapsing, Krystallus and his foe rolled down the slippery rocks into the shallow water. Dodging a punch, Krystallus kicked the elf in the chest, hard enough to send him sprawling backward into the waves. He spun around to face the other attackers.

Wham! The butt of a spear struck him hard on the temple.

Krystallus teetered, dazed. Then another sharp blow to the head knocked him over. He splashed into the shallows and lay there, facedown in the water.

22: THE CHOICE

How I love to gamble! To roll dice, to take a risk, to trust in luck. Especially when what's at stake belongs to someone else.

When Krystallus awoke, the feeling wasn't pleasant. His head throbbed, as if boulders were constantly slamming his skull. His stomach churned with swallowed seawater, and his mouth was rank with the stench of his own vomit. And his new surroundings didn't bode well.

He lay on the stone floor of some kind of cell. When, after much effort, he brought his eyes into focus, he looked at his tattered tunic and leggings—and checked for his precious sketchbook, which was still in his pocket. Around him he saw only stone walls, floor, and ceiling, unbroken but for a bolted door and a barred skylight high above his head. On the floor beside him were two items of furniture: a rickety stool and a bucket, made from a large seashell, that held some water.

Dazed and nauseated, he forced his wobbly limbs to crawl over to the bucket. Plunging his head into the water, he tried to rinse away the smell of retch. But even that small amount of effort was enough to cause the boulders to strike his skull again.

Head throbbing, feeling more dizzy than ever, he collapsed onto the stone floor. Then, despite his effort to resist, he vomited again. Seawater and shreds of kelp gushed out of his mouth, making a rancid puddle on the floor. Dark shadows crept into his mind, obscuring any thoughts. As the shadows deepened, he lost consciousness.

When he awoke again, the cell seemed darker than before. At first, he thought he was on the edge of losing consciousness again. Or had he somehow returned to the endless night of Shadowroot? Gradually, he realized that, no, this darkness lay outside himself. And it wasn't the constant, oppressive darkness of that dangerous realm. He was, judging from the sound of waves crashing somewhere beyond these walls, still in Waterroot.

Ignoring the continuous throbs in his head, he rolled over onto his back. That alone took all his strength. Through the skylight, he saw the dim glimmers of stars through the hazy air. He lay on the stones, panting from exertion.

Footsteps echoed in a corridor nearby. The heavy iron bolt in the door slid open. Krystallus closed his eyes, pretending to be still unconscious.

Booted feet entered the cell. Someone stepped over to him and roughly shoved his shoulder. It took all his self control for Krystallus to keep his eyes closed. Enraged, he wanted badly to leap to his feet and teach the intruder some manners. But he knew enough to resist. In his current condition, he probably couldn't even stand up, let alone challenge anyone to fight. He remained motionless on the floor, heart pounding.

"Looks like yer prisoner's still half dead," said a voice that sounded like river rocks grinding against each other.

"When he wakes up, he'll wish he was *totally* dead," another voice replied with a loud guffaw.

"Right as a rudder you are, mate! I hear the queen wants to see him the second he comes around."

The queen? thought Krystallus. *So she's alive?*

"Took a while to wake up herself, she did. But the healer told me that she woke up real fast when she heard how they caught him trying to strangle her. Her first command was 'bring him to me.'" Another guffaw. "And believe me, she ain't planning to serve him high tea."

"She looked madder 'n a hooked shark, she did! Saw her myself when I brung some healer goods to her royal chamber."

Someone kicked Krystallus on the thigh. He kept his eyes closed, trying not to wince.

"Leave him, now. Yer going to have other chances to kick him, I'll wager."

"Right." A loud guffaw. "After Serella has him shot, stabbed, drowned, and keelhauled."

Laughing raucously, the two elves left the cell. The door slammed and the iron bolt slid shut.

Hearing their bootsteps as they walked away, Krystallus opened his eyes. Above the fray of questions in his mind, he tried to focus all his attention on just one: How could he possibly escape?

Stone walls on every side, as well as above and below.

Nothing but a wooden stool and a big, bowl-shaped shell. What chance did he have to get out of this place before Serella had him killed?

None, he told himself morbidly. *Not even a ghost could get out of here.* He caught his breath. *Unless . . .*

Lifting his eyes to the skylight, he squinted up at the opening. Too high to jump. But maybe there was another way!

Rolling over on his side, he slowly pushed himself up to his knees, then his feet. Though his head swam dizzily, he managed to keep his balance long enough to totter over to the shell. He brought it to the center of the cell and turned it over, dumping out the remaining water. Grabbing the stool, he placed it on top of the upside-down shell. Without even testing this contraption for strength, he climbed onto the stool. Unsteady as he was, he managed to stand on top of the seat.

It held. Swaying precariously, head pounding, he stretched his arms upward, grasping for the skylight. There! One hand, then the other, wrapped around one of the iron bars.

Lifting his feet off the stool, he bounced vigorously, tugging with all his weight. The bar made a grinding noise, and a few chips of stone dropped onto his head. He shook them off, ignoring the hammering in his skull. Again he bounced, this time twisting the bar with all his strength.

Without warning, the bar broke loose. Krystallus crashed downward, along with the iron bar and a small avalanche of stone chips. Although he landed hard on the floor, his head barely missing the stool, he didn't care. Gazing upward, he grunted with satisfaction. A few more stars shone through the hole in the ceiling.

Hoping nobody had heard the crash, he hastily reassembled his makeshift ladder. With the first bar removed, it was much easier to take out three more. Then, hanging from the last remaining bar, Krystallus called on every drop of strength in his arms and hoisted himself up. With several kicks of his legs, all the while hoping the bar would hold, he pulled himself out of the hole.

Panting with exhaustion, he rested on his knees, inhaling the cold night air. After a moment, he began to survey his surroundings. He was on a low, flat rooftop, paved with slabs of sea-blue slate. The roof connected to a much larger building, made from enormous chunks of stone that looked greenish blue in the starlight. Directly above the junction of his rooftop and the building, a wide balcony adorned a row of vaulting archways that bordered a huge, brightly lit room— the great hall of the queen, he guessed.

Lifting his gaze higher, he traced the outline of the building. Even in the dark of night, he couldn't miss the lone turret that rose high above everything else. The turret was just large enough to hold one room, which would possess a commanding view of the ocean and sky.

Serella's room. I'm sure of it. He studied the turret, trying to see into the tall, narrow windows behind its wooden balcony. But all he could discern was the flickering light of a fire—her hearth, perhaps—somewhere within.

Turning away from the building, he scanned the open

ocean. Starlight glistened on rolling waves as far as he could see, making the water seem like a rippling, undulating reflection of the night sky. Below the outer edge of the rooftop, waves sloshed against the shore. And a few hundred paces down that shore, he could make out the flickering green flames of a portal.

Where I arrived, he noted. *Now, that was an impressive bit of navigation! To come out right here at Serella's home.* Patting his swollen temple, he added wryly, *And into the arms of her guards.*

He glanced back up at the austere, commanding turret, and shook his head. *All right, I should have guessed.* Serella surely ran this place as ruthlessly as she ran all her expeditions. She would tolerate no errors—and no forgiveness. That rule would apply to her people, as well as any visitors.

Just the sort of person you should be really sure you want to save before you try. Smirking, he shook his head. Then, unbidden, he recalled his surprising feelings when he'd thought she was dead . . . feelings that still lingered, brushing the edges of his mind like a distant ocean breeze. She was a person, maybe even a special person, worth saving.

He looked down the shoreline to the portal's green flames. That place guaranteed his escape, provided he moved quickly and stealthily. He should start right now, before the elves discovered his absence. And then hunted him down and brought him back to be skewered by their queen.

For several seconds he gazed at the portal. Then he slowly

turned back to the high turret and its luminous hearth. Drawing a deep breath, he rose to his feet and started to climb—not downward, toward safety, but upward, toward the turret.

There was someone up there he wanted to see.

23: UNEXPECTED GIFT

What I fear the most is what I know the least.

Minutes later, Krystallus pulled himself quietly over the railing of Queen Serella's balcony. He paused for a moment, listening to the constant slap of rolling waves far below, then crept stealthily closer to her room. Crouched by an open window, he could peer inside without being discovered.

What he saw confirmed his hopes. Polished driftwood lined every wall, holding dozens of shelves that sagged with countless treasures from Serella's travels. There were three precious firestones, glowing like molten lava, from Rahnawyn's volcanoes; a slab of singing wood from the groves of El Urien; and an airy looking flower, glowing pink, that might have come from the Cloud Gardens of Y Swylarna. In addition, there were intricate carvings, painted masks, strings of shining pearls, at least three jewel-studded swords, a magical kite that floated above its shelf without any wind, a jade harp fitted with strings of unicorn manes, seven massive volumes with golden runes on their bindings, an enormous bow and a quiver of arrows fletched with the orange feathers of trueflight hawks, a vial that bubbled with the potent juices of hynallawn berries, several jars of iridescent mud from the high plains of Malóch, an ogre's eyeball (floating in a clear glass bubble), a spiraling tusk of ivory from some creature he couldn't recognize, a more complex compass than he'd ever seen before, a shaggy but luxurious green scarf that must have been woven by the spider faeries of Crystillia, a rare piece of maroon amber that could—he'd heard—alter its color with every change of fortune, a large pile of beautifully wrought silver coins, the largest conch shell he'd ever seen, a crystal goblet with the lavender-scented water of the Elven River, a pile of tattered maps, and much more besides.

Not bad, he thought, feeling a surge of grudging admiration.

On one wall, a small fireplace sat inside a whalebone hearth. Behind a golden screen, fire burned vigorously, casting wavering light around the room. By the opposite wall sat a massive bed, whose frame and posts were decorated with colorful sea stars. On the bedpost nearest to the fire perched a small, silver-winged owlet. And under the mass of blue and green blankets, woven from the finest strands of deep sea kelp, lay Serella.

She was propped against several pillows, her silvery blond hair flowing past her pointed ears and down over her shoulders. Judging from the tray of food and drink on the table by her side, she had recently eaten. And judging from the sour expression on her face, she was not at all happy. Krystallus could tell that beyond any doubt. For she was, he suddenly realized, looking straight at him.

He started, nearly falling backward onto the balcony. She merely continued to gaze at him, firelight dancing in her deep green eyes.

"Well?" she asked hoarsely. "Are you going to come in or not?"

Krystallus stood, stepped over to a richly carved door, and turned the silver handle. He entered the queen's room, keeping his gaze locked on hers. Serella didn't budge, but as soon as he stepped inside, the owlet on the bed post clacked its beak loudly.

"Hush now, Clowella," she said with a glance at the owlet. Then, in a casual tone, she added, "He's just come here to kill me."

Krystallus scowled. "If I wanted to kill you, I wouldn't have taken the trouble of bringing you back from Lastrael. You were about to die when I found you." He peered at her face; the shadowy lines had almost disappeared. "Looks like your healers have done their work well."

Serella snorted disdainfully. "A likely story! My guards told me you were trying to strangle me when they arrived."

Shaking his head, Krystallus walked over to the floating kite and flicked it with his finger. It rose higher into the air, and even though there was no wind, made a graceful circle around the room before coming back to float above its shelf.

"Actually," he replied at last, "I was checking your pulse to see if you were still alive." He glared at her. "I thought you were dead. My second mistake."

Her eyebrows arched. "And what was your first?"

"Trying to save you," he answered coolly. Then, furrowing his brow, he asked, "How did you know I was out there on your balcony?"

She curled the corner of her mouth in a grin. "The maroon amber. It changed color."

Turning around, Krystallus saw that, indeed, the piece of amber on the shelf was no longer the maroon color he'd seen. Instead, it was an ominous shade of black, much like the landscape of Shadowroot.

"Impressive," he said as he turned back to face her. "But while I hate to disappoint you, I didn't come here to kill you. You may be an arrogant, ruthless tyrant and a treacherous competitor . . . but you didn't deserve to die on the ground in some faraway realm. And you don't deserve to die tonight."

For the first time since he'd entered her room, Serella blinked. Firelight cast flickering shadows on her face. "Then why *did* you come here? Surely you could have escaped by now. And my guards will—"

"Want to kill me, I know." He stepped calmly to the side of her bed. Ignoring the owlet, who was watching him closely, he bent closer to Serella. "You really want to know why I came?"

"Yes," she declared, but without her usual imperiousness. Eyes wide, she peered up at him. "Why?"

He bent lower and kissed her on the lips. She flinched in surprise, but didn't pull away. Instead, she placed her hands on the sides of his head and pulled him closer, kissing him passionately.

Finally, they separated. After a pause, Krystallus said, "That's why."

"You . . . you know . . ." She brushed back her hair, then cleared her throat. "That sort of impertinence could get you killed."

"Add it to my list of crimes," he said with a grin. He watched her for a few more seconds, then turned away, preparing to leave her chamber. He paused to glance at the piece of amber, whose color was now golden yellow.

"Wait," she said—not in the commanding voice of a queen, but in the beseeching voice of a lover. "I have something to give you." She almost smiled. "Something else, that is."

He turned and cocked his head questioningly.

"Over there," she said, pointing to an object on one of the shelves. "That compass. I want you to have it."

He shook his head of white hair. "But you *need* that. For your explorations."

"No," she said a bit sadly, "I think you need it more. Deserve it more, at any rate." She bit her lip, then continued. "Don't you understand why I taunted you all those times? Why I humiliated you every chance I could?"

Krystallus said nothing. He merely continued to meet her gaze.

"It was to prod you to be your own self! To step out of your father's shadow."

After a long pause, she added in a whisper, "You have started to do that. And now . . . you will be the greatest explorer Avalon has ever known." She grinned. "Except, of course, for me."

"Of course," he replied, grinning back. "But the compass—"

"Is yours. You saved my life—and besides, I want you to have it." Her eyes gleamed knowingly. "You'll find some uses for it, I'm sure."

Krystallus swallowed. He wanted to stride over and kiss her again, but resisting the impulse, he walked to the shelf and carefully removed the compass. Expertly crafted, it was shaped like a glass globe inside a leather strap. Within the globe, held in place by hair-thin wires, were a pair of silver arrows. Tilting the globe slightly, he gasped. For he'd just realized what this instrument could really do.

"One arrow points westward, as with all compasses," he observed. "To the heart of El Urien, first home of the elves." He glanced up at her. "Appropriately."

Looking back at the globe, he went on, "But the other arrow, the additional one—that spins on a vertical axis. So it always points *starward*."

Serella gave a nod. "So no matter where you are—under the root-realms, inside the trunk of the Great Tree, or anywhere else—you can always find your way."

Gratitude filled his heart, but he couldn't find the words to express it.

"Now," she said, "you can be the first explorer to climb all the way to the stars." With a mischievous gleam, she added, "Unless I get there first."

"Your challenge is accepted." More quietly, he said, "And so is your gift."

"Good. I wouldn't want anything bad to happen to you. You're my . . . favorite competitor."

Reminded of how he'd found her in Shadowroot, Krystallus grew suddenly serious. "You shouldn't go back to Lastrael. Something is very wrong about that place. What it did to you, and the elves with you, I've never seen anything like it."

Her expression turned somber. "I know. Something attacked us, all at once. The chief healer told me she thought it was a kind of plague—*darkdeath*, she called it."

"Darkdeath?"

"Right. But if that's true, it raises more questions than it answers. How does this plague spread? Who is susceptible—only elves, or everybody? How can it be prevented? I need to go back there to find out."

"No," he pleaded, waving his arm. "Don't risk it. Don't go back there."

Teasingly, she shot back, "Why? So you can discover all the wonders of that realm by yourself?"

"No," he answered, his voice gentle. "So nothing will harm my"—he paused, choosing his words—"favorite competitor."

She beamed at him. "All right, then. I won't go. That is, until I change my mind."

"The right of every queen." He gave her a mock bow. "But first, I—"

Bootsteps, growing louder by the second, interrupted him. They were pounding up the stairs that led to the top of the turret.

"My guards," said Serella, heaving a sigh. "They are coming to tell me you've escaped."

"It won't please them to find me here with you." Looking over at the amber, he saw the golden color darkening swiftly. "They might think I'm here to murder you."

"Or to steal a kiss."

Krystallus almost grinned, but the pounding grew louder. Now the guards were only seconds away. He started toward the balcony, then paused and glanced back at her. "I'm glad I didn't kill you."

Her voice a whisper, she replied, "So am I."

Krystallus ran to the door and climbed over the balcony railing, just as three armed guards burst into the queen's chamber. Although he couldn't hear all their jumbled, breathless words, he couldn't help but chuckle when he heard Serella's harsh reprimand: "You *what?* You let him escape?"

Stealthily, he climbed back down the building wall, pressing his toes into the gaps between stones. The compass, safe in his tunic's breast pocket, almost seemed to touch his heart.

24: A PROMISE

Sometimes a victory has the look and smell of a total loss.

Basilgarrad flew swiftly, shearing the tops of high, bulbous clouds with his wings. Spread wide, those wings glistened, each of their thousands of green scales covered with mist from the clouds, each of their powerful muscles rimmed with rivers of vapor. With every rhythmic beat, sheets of droplets poured off the wings' rear edges, forming trailing veils that shimmered with rainbows.

But the dragon wasn't enjoying this flight back to Woodroot. Not at all. Not even the feeling of Merlin atop his head, leaning into the wind with an arm around his great friend's ear, gave Basilgarrad any comfort.

Ever since they had left the scene of the blight and returned Rhia, Lleu, and Nuic to their home at the Society's compound, he'd felt an ominous weight swelling inside of him. It dragged on his wings, just as it weighed heavily on every thought, crushing his hopes like a blight of the mind.

That shadow beast! he raged silently. From the very moment he'd seen its writhing shape in Bendegeit's sphere, he couldn't dispel the feeling that it was growing stronger by the day. That it was behind all Avalon's troubles. And that it was laughing at him—raucously laughing—for his failure to stop its plans.

I don't even know what it is, he grumbled, *let alone where it is. We're no better off than before I went to Bendegeit's lair!*

"Not true," replied Merlin, who had overheard his thoughts. Speaking directly into the dragon's ear, he said, "We know now, thanks to you, that there is one central source of all this wickedness. We don't know what, or where, it is— that's true. But we will find it! That's certain."

Yet even the wizard's encouraging words didn't lift Basilgarrad's mood. As he sailed through another bank of clouds, scattering luminous mist in his wake, he ground his massive jaws together, scraping hundreds of titanic teeth.

All I know is that beast is evil. Wholly evil. The phrase that had come to him when he'd seen it returned, echoing in his mind: *Darker than dark.*

He banked to one side, tilting from the tip of his snout to the club of his tail, to avoid an especially dark cloud. Lightning sizzled and sparked inside of it. Rumbling thunder filled the air, resounding like the shadow beast's laughter.

Why can't I shake the feeling I've met that beast before?

"Try thinking about something else, old sport," counseled the voice in his ear. "Something more pleasant. How about that irrepressible dragon maiden you met in Waterroot? The one who wanted to fly?"

Basilgarrad shook his head, nearly knocking Merlin over. Not even the memory of Marnya could distract him right now from his worries. For those worries concerned something much greater than himself: Avalon, this unique and fragile world.

Merlin sighed, making a somber wind that filled the dragon's ear. "I understand, my friend. I'm just as worried! When I saw Rhia's suit of vines restored to its old vitality, that lifted my spirits—as did her yelp of joy when I asked her to keep the crystal of élano. But those brief moments didn't last long. My mood's been as dark as could be. As dark as that *thing* you saw."

Beneath him, the dragon shuddered. Merlin wondered aloud, "Maybe this visit with Hallia will help! And maybe the sight of your favorite forest will do the same."

The first glimpse of Woodroot's groves appeared, a patchwork quilt of greenery threaded with mist. As they burst out of the clouds, Basilgarrad caught the scent of lilac from the purple-hued trees of the Fairlyn Valley. Without thinking about it, he created his own smell of lilacs, magnifying the aroma from below. Yet even this experience couldn't banish the lingering shadows from his mind.

"There!" cried Merlin. "Down on that meadow."

Instantly, Basilgarrad veered left, knowing just what the wizard had seen. A herd of deer bounded gracefully through the grass of an open meadow. He glided steadily lower. Even before he landed at the meadow's edge, one of the deer—a long-limbed doe with unusually large eyes—broke away from the herd and started running toward them, her hooves practically flying over the grass.

Merlin quickly climbed down from his perch, using Basil's ear as a bendable ladder. The doe, meanwhile, bounded closer. As they watched, she began to metamorphose. Graceful forelegs shortened into arms, hind legs pulled upright, and the deer's torso lifted vertically. At the same time, her neck and chin shortened, her ears shrank, her head sprouted an auburn braid, while her tan fur melted into a brown tunic. As the doe, now fully transformed into Hallia, strode toward them, only her wide brown eyes remained unchanged.

The wizard opened his arms to embrace her. To his own surprise, Basilgarrad watched them with uncommon interest. His heart beat faster; his long neck bent their way. Why, he couldn't explain. Certainly, it had nothing to do with that water dragon Marnya! Whatever the reason, he watched the reunited couple hug and kiss, then amble over to a bubbling stream that coursed through the meadow.

The celebratory mood swiftly vanished as Merlin told Hallia about all their struggles. The troubles in Fireroot—with greedy dragons as well as dwarves as stubborn as Zorgat, who had broken his obsidian arrow. The violent dispute of the birds on the cloud bridge. The frightful journey to the secret lake of élano—and their victory, temporarily at least, over the blight. And Basilgarrad's ominous discovery in the lair of the highlord of the water dragons.

"What does all this mean?" asked Hallia, her hands on her cheeks. "How do we end these troubles once and for all?"

Merlin gazed for a moment into the splashing stream, then shook his head. "I really don't know." He waved in the direction of Basil. "Nor does he, I'm afraid."

But I will find the answer, promised the dragon silently.

I know you will, my friend, Merlin replied. Yet even in telepathy, he didn't sound convinced.

Abruptly, Hallia's back straightened. She clenched her jaw like a doe determined to protect her fawn. "Next time you go anywhere—anywhere at all—I want to go with you."

Merlin took her hand. "No, Hallia, no. The dangers, the risks—it's not safe. No."

She pulled her hand away. Sternly, she said, "You take your sister, Rhia, on risky journeys, through portals and even deep underground! Why not me?"

"Well, I . . ." he began.

"Yes?" she asked, raising an eyebrow. "Am I any less deserving than Rhia? Am I any less important to you?"

Impressed, Basilgarrad cocked his ears forward. *Smart creatures, those females.*

Too smart, shot back Merlin. *She has me trapped! What can I do?*

Give in, advised the dragon.

No! he protested. To Hallia, he began, "But—"

"There is nothing to discuss," she said curtly. "Either I'm just as important to you, or not."

Merlin frowned, peering at her. "All right," he agreed.

"The next journey, so long as it's not utterly foolhardy, I will bring you."

You realize, said the dragon telepathically, *that rules out almost all our journeys.* But Merlin ignored him.

Hallia, though, seemed pleased. Taking his hand again, she said, "That's all I want."

"All *I* want," he replied, "is that you stay safe." He grimaced. "I couldn't bear—"

"Shhhhh." She placed a finger on his lips. "That won't happen." Then she leaned forward. "To either of us, my hawk." She smiled at him, and it was a smile of true devotion.

Well done, great wizard. Basil bent one of his ears, imitating a bow. *You knew right when to surrender.*

Merlin glanced his way and gave him a wink.

She vanquished you just now.

The wizard grinned ever so slightly. *She did that a long time ago.*

All of them turned as a rough squawking filled the air. A ragged black bird approached, flying erratically over the meadow. It held a slender object in its claws. Merlin, Hallia, and Basilgarrad watched the bird as it crashed, exhausted, on the grass beside them.

"Zorgat's dwarf raven!" exclaimed Merlin, leaping to his feet.

Hallia, meanwhile, cupped her hands in the cold water of the stream and brought the bird a drink. It plunged its beak into the tiny pool and drank avidly.

Basilgarrad's nostrils flared. "And look what it brought."

Merlin's eyes focused on the slender object the raven had carried all the way from Fireroot. "Zorgat's arrow!" He traded glances with Basil. "The shaft has been repaired!"

"He must be ready to discuss a treaty with the dragons," declared Basilgarrad. He thumped the meadow with his gargantuan tail, causing the stream to splash over its banks. "There may still be hope for Fireroot."

The dwarf raven released a loud squawk.

Merlin bent down and picked up his staff, which he'd set beside the stream. Straightening, he met Hallia's gaze. "Are you ready for that journey?"

She nodded eagerly.

He placed his hand on her shoulder, "This could be our chance to turn the tide—in Fireroot, at least. And if we can restore the peace there, perhaps we can do it everywhere, all across Avalon!" His bushy brows drew together, forming a dark bramble above his eyes. "Any sign of danger, though, and you must leave."

"Fair enough," she replied.

"That's easy to accomplish," chimed in Basilgarrad. "At any sign of danger, I want to leave, too."

Merlin squinted at him. "Some dragon you are," he teased.

Basilgarrad's tone turned serious. "Just a dragon who prefers peace to war."

Merlin looked into the enormous green eyes of his friend. "So do we all," he said somberly. "So do we all."

25: TORCHLIGHT

Danger, like fire, can warm a man's hands or cook food on his hearth—until it leaps up and destroys his house.

Basilgarrad thrust his head into the tunnel, crumpling his huge ears. He winced as they pushed against some painfully sharp amethyst crystals.

Curse that bone-brained Zorgat and his desire for secrecy! the dragon fumed to himself. *Who in his right mind would hold a meeting like this underground?*

From deep in his throat, he released an angry rumble. *Humiliating! I bring everybody here, including that ungrateful raven—and what do I get? A seat barely big enough for my nose.* His eyes narrowed. *If only I could breathe fire . . . I'd light Zorgat's beard!*

Merlin, who was standing several paces away in the center of the jewel-studded cavern, with Hallia at his side, glanced over at his friend's huge face. For a moment he studied the dragon, whose eyes and scales shone brightly in the light from all the torches that lined the walls. Even though that face was jammed inside the tunnel, it clearly showed Basilgarrad's great intelligence, sensitivity—and frustration.

The wizard sighed. *I understand, old chap. But I'm glad, all the same, you can't destroy Zorgat's beard. It took him his whole life to grow, you know.*

I suppose you're right, thought Basil unhappily. He shifted his head a bit, breaking off a few dozen amethyst crystals that clattered on the floor like purple hail. *But it's still tempting!*

Just then Zorgat stamped his boot on the floor of the torchlit cavern. Flanked by thirty or forty dwarves, his arms folded over his bristly beard, the dwarves' chief elder gave Merlin and Hallia a deep bow. The small raven on his shoulder fluttered its tattered black wings to keep its balance, but Zorgat didn't seem to notice. His face, etched with wrinkles, showed only grave seriousness. When he stood straight again, he spoke first to Hallia.

"A true honor it is to meet you, esteemed woman of the deer people." His eyes, as bright as the jewels adorning the cavern walls, sparkled. "I have heard many tales, but never met one of your clan before."

Hallia curtseyed gracefully. "The honor is wholly mine, chief elder." She glanced at Merlin and smiled. "But you should give the credit to my husband, for it was his idea to bring me."

Merlin's eyebrows lifted, but he said nothing. His thoughts were focused on the dwarf leader. Would Zorgat keep his word? What would be his terms? Would the dragons ever agree to them?

Zorgat turned to Merlin. "When you last were here, you

left me with a broken arrow—as well as an idea, no less severed than this shaft."

From his wide leather belt, lined with dark red rubies, he drew the mended arrow. Slowly, he turned it, making the obsidian blade flash in the torchlight. "Now the arrow has been mended. Let us hope it will stand the strain of being put to use."

Somewhere in the row behind him, a dwarf grumbled angrily. Zorgat whirled around, peering at his people. His tone severe, he snarled, "For the last time, hear me! This decision stands. Dangerous as it will be to try to work with the fire dragons—it is even more dangerous to battle them constantly. That is my decision! Does any one dare object?"

None of the dwarves spoke. Some of them shook their bearded heads. Others bowed respectfully. But a few, Basilgarrad noticed with concern, fingered the double-bladed axes in their belts or the bows and arrows on their shoulders.

"Need I remind you," Zorgat pressed, "how many of our people we lost only last week in that mine collapse—something that the broad backs of dragons could have prevented? Are we dwarves so set in our ways that we will refuse to try a new idea?"

Again, no dwarves answered.

Merlin, his expression hopeful, traded glances with the green dragon. *Perhaps, Basil, all our hard work in this fiery realm might finally amount to something.*

Zorgat gazed intently at the wizard. "So be it," he declared. "If you can persuade the fire dragons to adopt this treaty, with no treachery, we will work together with them in all our mines except the sacred caverns of the flaming jewels. For their labors to secure shafts and melt down ore, we will reward them with one third of whatever treasure we mine."

Merlin's brow furrowed. "They will ask for two thirds, you know."

The dwarf stroked his beard, a canny gleam in his eyes. "Then we shall protest loudly, decry their greed—and reluctantly settle at half for each of us."

Merlin nodded. "An excellent plan."

"And to prevent treachery," Zorgat added, "we shall seek—"

"I have already discussed the matter with Basilgarrad," finished the wizard, pointing the tip of his staff toward the gargantuan face jammed into the tunnel. "He has agreed to bring his personal vengeance down on any fire dragons who violate the treaty."

Basilgarrad's head nodded slightly, breaking off another avalanche of amethyst crystals. "Gladly," he declared, his voice echoing inside the cavern.

"Then," declared Zorgat, "it is agreed. By us, at least. Now we must win over the fire dragons."

Merlin twisted his staff, grinding it into the floor. "I will help, chief elder, with all my skill."

"That is enough for me," Zorgat replied, his weathered old face showing at least a glimmer of hope.

Hallia, during this exchange, gazed around the cavern. Her heart swelled to see Merlin, her husband and dearest friend, making such historic progress. This could be the start of a whole new era! At least in one realm. And she, herself, was here to witness it.

She savored the scene: the dwarves all standing in line, grim yet expectant; the torches blazing, their fires reflected in the crystalline walls; Merlin and Zorgat facing each other with shared respect. *Yes, yes,* she thought, *I'm very glad I came.*

At the very edge of her vision, she saw a sudden movement. Possessing a deer's acute sensitivity to danger, she quickly turned—and gasped. There, at the end of the row, one black-bearded dwarf had raised his bow and nocked an arrow, preparing to shoot. His target, she saw clearly, was Merlin!

Even as she gasped, the dwarf released his obsidian-tipped arrow. The bowstring twanged and the arrow flew—straight at Merlin's chest. There was no time to warn him, no time to shout his name, no time to do anything.

Except . . .

Hallia instantly shifted into the shape of a deer. Her hooves dug into the cavern floor, scraping against the stone, as her powerful hind legs threw her into a desperate leap. A fraction of a second before the arrow struck its intended target, Hallia's body passed before it. The arrow plunged deep into her ribs. With a cry of pain, she collapsed to the floor, blood pouring from the wound.

Pandemonium erupted. Nearby dwarves pounced on the assailant, pummeling him. The whole cavern trembled as Merlin shouted, dwarves cursed, and Basilgarrad roared in anguish. "Traitor!" bellowed Zorgat, drawing his own bow and arrow. The dwarf raven on his shoulder leaped into the air and flew in circles above the fray, screeching madly.

By the time Zorgat reached the assailant, he lay unconscious on the floor. His bow lay smashed beside him. A trickle of blood stained his beard. No one, not even the elder, noticed the black leech sucking greedily on the dwarf's neck.

Merlin, meanwhile, sat on the hard floor, holding Hallia gently as she shifted back to her woman's body. He uttered a frenzied chant, making the arrow in her ribs vanish completely, leaving only a thin trail of dust in the air that sparkled momentarily and then drifted away. Calling on all his power, he started to probe her wound with his inner eye, hoping to knit her torn tissues back together. All around the cavern, torches flickered, their light dimming, as if the wizard was drawing their energy as well as his own.

He cried out in agony. It wasn't working! He couldn't see deep enough—too much damage, too much blood. And he knew, beyond doubt, that the arrow had pierced her heart.

"No . . . my hawk," she said hoarsely. "It's too . . . late."

"No, Hallia!" His whole body quaked as he drew a breath. "What good is being a wizard if I can't help you now?"

Her doe eyes, warm and deep and brown, gazed up at him. "I'll always . . . love you." She caught her breath, twisting in a spasm of pain. Her eyes closed briefly, then reopened.

"Someday . . . we'll run together . . . again. Two deer . . . side by side . . . in the meadows . . . of the Otherworld."

Face contorted, he slowly nodded. His lips parted to speak, but no words came.

As torches wavered weakly all around the cavern, Hallia fell limp in Merlin's arms.

26: THE GREEN HEART OF AVALON

Words ought to be chosen with greater care than either clothing or weaponry. For they can last much longer than the former, and cut far deeper than the latter.

From every realm, the mourners came. Singly or in groups, by wings or feet or hooves, sobbing or silent, they gathered at the innermost meadow of the Summerlands, the place deer people called *the green heart of Avalon*. On this day, however, the grass, touched by autumn's first chill, was more auburn than green.

The wind gusted briskly, blowing leaves of maple, oak, and birch across the meadow. Basilgarrad, seated near the trees, somberly watched them bending under the weight of the wind. He wondered for a moment if his old friend Aylah, the wind sister, had come to join the mourners. *No*, he concluded, *wherever Aylah is today, she's not here.*

He watched as people of all kinds approached Merlin. Wearing a simple black tunic, the wizard stood by the mossy bank of a spring that bubbled out of the ground, forming a green-rimmed pool. This was, he knew, one of Hallia's favorite places, a spot where Merlin and his bride had shared many a night under the stars.

Some of the mourners, like the dreamfinder elf from the Swaying Sea who had seven fingers on each hand and walked with a limp, were unfamiliar to Basilgarrad. Others, like the tall mudmaker Aelonnia of Isenwy and the cloudlike sylph who floated across the meadow, he recognized from Merlin and Hallia's wedding years before. And others he knew well—at least well enough to feel their sorrow. There was Rhia, who gave her brother a tearful embrace. And Nuic, whose lifeless gray color said more than any words the sprite could have spoken. There was Shim, whose thunderous steps rocked the meadow. Zorgat the dwarf came, too, looking much older and stricken with grief. And there was Gwynnia—who had been nursed back to health, as a young dragon, by Hallia herself.

Gwynnia trudged slowly across the grass, leaving a flattened trail that glistened with silvery dragon tears. Though much smaller than Basilgarrad, with her wings folded tightly against her back, she still exuded a dragon's majesty and power as she moved. And a dragon's sheer bulk, as well—which is why she needed to take care not to crush anyone with her tail. Following close behind her came Ganta, her son. The little dragon's orange eyes flashed when his gaze met Basilgarrad's. Perhaps he felt suddenly afraid, or perhaps he was still pondering his uncle's strange words about the true meaning of bigness. That was impossible to tell.

Only one group of guests did not approach Merlin: the

deer people of Hallia's clan, the Mellwyn-bri-Meath. Like Basilgarrad, they had shared their sadness with Merlin earlier. For now they were content to stand together, like a herd of deer, watching in silence from the edge of the meadow.

Some of them, Basilgarrad noticed, stood in their deer forms—at least one broad-chested stag and several graceful does. Or were those really the deer people's cousins, the true deer who lived in these glades? A few deer folk seemed to have a misty, translucent appearance, as if they had traveled all the way from their people's ancient home in Lost Fincayra—the land of the fabled Carpet Caerlochlann, whose every thread was made from the deer folk's most treasured stories.

Krystallus, the last person to arrive, stepped onto the meadow. He barely glanced at his father and spoke to no one, choosing to stand alone by a group of birch trees. Head bowed, his white hair obscuring his face, he seemed so isolated he might have been standing in another realm.

When, at last, everyone who wished to speak with Merlin had done so, the wizard bent down and lifted something from the grass—a specially crafted bowl. Made from shards of deer hooves and antlers, it glistened with the subtle magic of Hallia's people. Within it sat a small, silvery mound—Hallia's remains, after she'd been cremated in the traditional style of the deer people.

Holding the bowl against his chest, so that he could feel its weight against him, Merlin spoke. Although his voice was the rough whisper of a man who had talked too much in recent days, his words rang out across the grass.

"We will miss you, Hallia, always and forever." He paused to swallow. "Wherever your spirit roams . . . may you find green meadows. Deep glades. And loving hearts."

With that, he raised the bowl and flung the silvery ashes into the air. Taken by the wind, the ashes rose high, like a leaping doe whose hooves might never again touch the ground. Then, with the grace of a gentle rain, they drifted downward, alighting on the clear pool, the swaying trees, and the auburn grass.

The ashes landed, as well, upon everyone who had gathered in Hallia's memory. One silver fleck landed on one of Basilgarrad's eyelashes. He blinked, sending it floating over to the very tip of his enormous nose. At the instant it touched down, he felt a warm, stirring sensation—as if Hallia herself had laid her hand upon him and wished him well.

Slowly, with the sweeping breeze, the mourners departed. One by one they left, voices silent. Soon no one remained except Merlin, still standing by the spring, and Basilgarrad, still watching him, as silent as any dragon can be. Plus . . . one more person.

Krystallus, finally, lifted his head. He looked across the meadow at his father—and his expression was not sorrow or sympathy. No, as Basilgarrad could tell right away, it was something else entirely: rage.

Quaking with anger, Krystallus strode over to the wizard, his boots crushing the grass underfoot. His fists were clenched, as if poised to strike. But he hit his father, instead, with words.

"You said it was wrong, terribly dangerous, for me to bring her to Fireroot. Yet it was fine for you, the great wizard, to do the same thing?"

"Krystallus, I—"

"Don't give me any of your excuses!" the young man bellowed. "I've heard enough for a lifetime."

Merlin, looking stricken, tried again. "But she asked—she begged . . ."

"I don't care," Krystallus declared, cutting him off. A gust of wind twirled his white mane and blew it over one of his shoulders, the way his mother had often worn her hair. "The fact is, you were right about the danger. Yes, right! But you chose to ignore that danger for your own selfish reasons." His voice dropped to a growl. "And as a result, you killed her. Not somebody's arrow. *You.*"

Merlin staggered, as if struck by a hammer. "My— my son . . ."

"Don't call me your son! I don't want to be that, ever again. Consider us, from this day onward—"

"Don't, Krystallus," bellowed the dragon, shaking his enormous head. But the young man ignored him.

"Strangers."

Krystallus turned abruptly and strode away across the meadow. He soon vanished into the trees, leaving no visible sign he'd ever been there. But the final word he had spoken seemed to hang in the air, refusing to depart.

Basilgarrad, looking at the anguished face of his friend, knew that it never would.

27: READY

When I think back to those days with Merlin, I realize that his most predictable quality was, alas, unpredictability.

Basilgarrad was not surprised when, after that brutal experience in the Summerlands, Merlin decided to spend some time alone. Nor was he surprised that his friend chose to climb Hallia's Peak, a place rich with memories. But he was very surprised how long the wizard stayed up there on the snowy slopes—seven whole weeks.

During that time, Basilgarrad did his best to continue the work he and Merlin had been doing as a team. The dragon rushed from realm to realm, resolving a dispute between two families of wyverns, preventing the destruction of a village by gobsken, and stopping the vengeful Lo Valdearg from organizing yet another attack on the dwarves. All these forays succeeded, but it was hard and lonely work, even for the creature now known throughout Avalon as Wings of Peace. Especially since he continued to feel, day and night, the chill of that evil shadow he'd seen in Bendegeit's lair—a shadow he still could not identify.

At last, on a crisp autumn day, Basilgarrad heard a familiar voice speaking inside his mind. It came as he was flying low across Woodroot's treetops, checking to make sure that no sign of blight had returned to his beloved forest. Since he was flying into a strong headwind, the air rushed past his ears and coursed over his wings, sounding like a gusty storm. Below him the branches, tossed about by the tempest, swished and cracked loudly. Even so, he had no trouble hearing Merlin's thoughts.

Hello there, Basil. How would you like to join me up here on Hallia's Peak? I'm on the west side, at the Stargazing Stone.

There was a new rush of wind in Basilgarrad's ears as he banked a sharp turn. *I'm on my way.*

Yet while his heart leaped with gladness to hear the wizard's voice again, he couldn't shake the feeling that something was wrong. Very wrong. Or was it just another brush of that elusive shadow?

A few moments later, he swooped out of the high, layered clouds above Stoneroot's towering peaks. His dragon's wings stretched nearly across the slope, dwarfing the boulders below. Yet he couldn't miss seeing one particular slab of stone. On it stood a tall, bearded man, looking as sturdy as the stone itself.

Seeing the dragon approach, Merlin raised his staff in greeting. As Basilgarrad landed, crushing dozens of lichen-covered rocks under his weight, the wizard stepped back to avoid the spray of pebbles and shredded lichen. When the enormous body came to a halt and the grinding stones had settled, Merlin said wryly, "You always did know how to make an entrance."

"I learned that from you," teased the dragon.

But Merlin didn't smile. In a tone both affectionate and sad, he said, "It's good to see you again, Basil." Leaning against his staff, he studied his friend, then added, "Before I must go."

"Go?" bellowed the dragon, loud enough that several rocks broke loose from the ledges below and clattered down the slope. "You only just returned!"

"Yes, I know," said Merlin softly. His eyes fell to the Stargazing Stone, where they traced some of the constellations that had been etched into the rock's surface. One constellation held his attention longer than the rest—the luminous row of stars, visible almost everywhere in Avalon, which people called the Wizard's Staff. "But I have decided, after much thought, that I must go."

"Where? Why?"

"Well . . ." The mage paused, twirling some of the wilder hairs of his bushy beard. "The time has come for me to leave Avalon."

"Leave Avalon!" roared Basilgarrad, with such force that a flock of geese high overhead suddenly scattered, breaking formation as birds flapped away in all directions. "You can't do that. Not now—when so much is going wrong! Our world—our home—is falling apart!"

"Not so, Basil." The wizard took a step closer on the boulder, gazing up into the dragon's immense eye. "I've been hearing tales of your successes, even as I've been grieving for Hallia. From the birds, from the pinnacle sprites, and also from Rhia, who came here to see me. All of them told me about the marvelous work of a dragon called Wings of Peace."

Basilgarrad shook his mighty head. "I managed, it's true, but not nearly as well as I would have done with you." His brow wrinkled, forming deep rifts between the scales. "Besides, that's not the point. Avalon's troubles are as great as ever! These outbreaks of violence aren't stopping. And I'm still no closer to finding that evil shadow beast. Merlin, you can't leave now!"

"Basil," said the wizard as he twisted his staff on the boulder, "what if these outbreaks really are just what I thought they were when they first appeared—the normal growing pains of a new world? What if they are, in fact, an important part of Avalon's growth? A chance for the people of this world to come together and learn to triumph over all their worst qualities: hatred, intolerance, and greed. Just think of it, Basil! That triumph would make Avalon's experiment all the more remarkable, all the more successful."

The dragon bared his teeth, snarling at this notion. Hundreds of sword-sharp teeth gleamed, as a deep rumble rose from his throat, shaking the surrounding boulders. "What happened to your vision of this world, the *Avalon idea*?"

"That idea is still as powerful as ever! Even more, if our precious world can find the way to rise above these troubles. Don't you see? What I was missing before was that true peace—the idea's highest form—comes not from a wizard who *imposes* peace, but from a world that *embraces* peace."

Basilgarrad's rumble grew louder. "Meanwhile, too many people will suffer and die. And Merlin—that shadow beast is still out there somewhere."

"Maybe so," the wizard agreed. "But have you considered the possibility that it's not here in Avalon?"

"Not here?"

"Yes! What if all this is a ruse, a clever distraction, designed to keep both of us constantly searching these realms?" His dark eyes sparkled with a new idea. "What if that wicked beast isn't in Avalon, after all? That would explain why nobody—not you, not I, not anyone—has seen it."

"That's madness!" thundered the dragon. "Where else could it be?"

Merlin leaned forward, lowering his voice to a whisper. "Earth. That's where."

"What? You can't be serious."

"Oh, but I am." Ignoring his friend's doubtful expression, the wizard explained, "Dagda told me, long ago, that the fate of these two worlds, Avalon and Earth, are deeply intertwined. Now, that mortal world is unlike Avalon in many ways—in its landscape, its people, and even its time, which moves at a different pace. But it is, like Avalon, a world of free will. A world of many wonders. And also . . . a world that the warlord Rhita Gawr covets greedily."

Basilgarrad, still unconvinced, cocked his ears toward the wizard. "So you have decided to go to Earth?"

Merlin nodded, as a mountain breeze tousled his hair. "It may be far away in distance, but not in destiny. Maybe the shadow beast is really there, plotting against us!" He paused, then added, "Besides, it's time to keep a promise I once made—to help a young king named Arthur create a place of peace, Camelot, on the war-torn isle of Britannia. It's a remarkable, inspiring idea."

"So is Avalon!" The dragon lifted his gigantic tail and slammed it, full force, into the mountainside. Snowy cornices broke off the ridge, avalanches careered down the slopes, and boulders crashed into the trees below. Birds rose into the sky, screeching and squawking angrily.

Basilgarrad waited for the din and tremors to cease. Then, peering closely at his longtime friend, he asked in a quieter voice, "Are you sure that's why you want to leave? Because there is important work in that faraway world?" His emerald eyes flashed. "Or because . . . the pain is just too great for you in this one?"

The wizard, caught off guard, looked down at the Stargazing Stone. For several seconds, he gazed at the etched constellations. Finally, he raised his head and answered with a single word.

"Both." He swallowed, then said shakily, "I just can't bear to stay here, Basil. Not now. I've lost"—his voice dropped to a ragged whisper—"too much."

The dragon, feeling Merlin's heartache, narrowed his green eyes. "But Avalon needs you. Now more than ever! You are its protector."

"No," the wizard replied, shaking his head. "Avalon has all the protection it needs—in you."

"Me?" Basilgarrad's entire body jerked, knocking more boulders down the slope.

"Yes. You."

For a long moment, the dragon scrutinized him. Then he said, in a voice that seemed very small for such an immense creature, "But . . . I'm not ready."

"Oh, but you are!" Merlin stepped closer on the stone. "You have been ready ever since you first hatched from your egg, even though you were smaller than my little finger and completely unaware of your own identity."

Seeing the doubt showing on every scale of the dragon's face, he continued. "That's why Dagda recognized how special you were right away. Why he sent Aylah to watch over you. And why he chose you to defend me against the kreelix."

The enormous brow furrowed. "I still don't understand why he chose me, out of all the creatures in Avalon. It's just as much of a mystery as why he told me to swallow a grain of sand from every realm."

Merlin gazed up at him, while a cool breeze rippled the sleeves of his tunic. "I don't know Dagda's reasons for giving you that command. But I do know this: He did have reasons. Good ones! You can trust in that." With a wave of his hand, he added, "Maybe it was because, more than any other creature alive, you *are* Avalon. The living embodiment of this world. Its hopes, its wonders, its—"

"Fears," finished the dragon somberly.

"That, too. But hear me, Basil. You are ready."

The dragon sighed, breathing a blast of air that almost

knocked the mage over backward. Then, as Merlin steadied himself with his staff, Basilgarrad asked, "Will you be coming back? Or are you leaving us . . . for good?"

"I really don't know. Probably I won't ever come back. That's part of what I've been doing these weeks up here. Saying good-bye"—he glanced at the summit of Hallia's Peak—"to Avalon."

Seeing all the stress on Merlin's face, especially in the creases around his eyes, Basilgarrad nodded glumly. He understood, for the first time, the full weight—and contrary pulls—of the wizard's true name Olo Eopia. It wasn't easy to be a *man of many worlds, many times.* Nor was it easy, in any world or time, to be so racked by loss and grief.

Merlin raised his tangled eyebrows, as he often did before saying something difficult. "And now, old chap, I must say good-bye to you." He stepped to the edge of the stone and placed his hand on the dragon's lower lip. "Just because I'm leaving this world, you know, doesn't mean I'm leaving *you.* We have something precious, more precious than any magic or any jewels, and that will never change. I promise! Even though I will be far away, I will be with you—for as long as the stars shine bright over Avalon."

Peering into the wizard's face, Basilgarrad frowned, forming deep ruts on his scaly brow. For the first time since he'd become a dragon, he felt very small indeed.

28: STARLIGHT

Ah, for a good night's sleep! I do recall having one of those . . .
ages ago. It's not the occasional bad dream I'm talking about.
It's waking up and seeing something worse than any dream.

Good-bye, my friend."

With those words, Merlin departed, calling on his power of Leaping to take him to another world. Basilgarrad sadly watched him fade away, dissolving into the sparkling air. At one moment there stood a wizard with his staff, gazing at the dragon from the Stargazing Stone; at the next moment, the slab of stone was empty.

Almost. Even after Merlin disappeared, for a few seconds his staff remained. Upright it stood, quivering amidst the magical sparks. Basilgarrad studied it, recalling Merlin's belief that it possessed a kind of intelligence, a mysterious will of its own. Slowly, as he watched, the staff began to fade away. Then, at the final instant, one of the runes carved on its shaft flashed in a burst of green light—and the staff vanished completely.

Strange, he thought, cocking his ears in puzzlement. *That wasn't the symbol for Leaping.* He knew that rune well: a star within a circle, which Merlin had gained, long before, in the Quest of the Seven Songs. No, to his surprise, the rune that had flashed was the one shaped like a dragon's tail.

Despite his sadness, Basilgarrad almost smiled. For he sensed, beyond doubt, that the staff had just told him farewell.

Stretching his enormous wings, he decided to spend the night on this slope by the Stargazing Stone. He nestled himself into the mountainside, knocking over several pinnacles and sending dozens of boulders crashing downward. Although it wasn't the most comfortable spot, he wanted to remain here, high on the rocky ridge of Hallia's Peak, accompanied only by his thoughts.

A few hours later, he woke with a start. Avalon's stars illuminated the sky, painting the surrounding peaks with lovely, ethereal light. Yet something felt *wrong* . . . enough to make his dragon's heart pound in his chest, jostling the granite boulders beneath him. Was it the sorrow he felt at Merlin's departure? The dread that he couldn't possibly save Avalon alone? Or the lingering fear that somewhere out there, a shadowy being was growing more powerful?

To calm himself, he turned to the Stargazing Stone. Thanks to the wizard's touch, the etchings of constellations glowed on the rock, mirror images of the real ones high above. Deliberately, he traced the shapes of the constellations—first on the stone, then in the sky. There was Pegasus, galloping across the horizon. Above, he saw the bright, rippling waters of the Stream of Light. And to the west, the starry meadows that held the Twisted Tree.

Basilgarrad turned to the Wizard's Staff—the most celebrated constellation in Avalon, and a special favorite of Merlin's. His nostrils suddenly flared. He roared in dismay, a roar that echoed across the peaks and woke many a creature to the same terrible discovery.

The stars of the Wizard's Staff were gone! At the place in the sky where they had glowed since the very birth of Avalon—nothing remained. Nothing but bottomless holes of blackness.

Once again, the dragon roared. The sound, fierce yet forlorn, made even the mountains quake. At last, it faded away into the night.

In the weeks and months that followed, disasters mounted, spreading across the seven realms like a new kind of blight. Basilgarrad raced to every trouble spot, but even his broad wings couldn't hold back the rising tide of violence. Tensions between Fireroot's dwarves and dragons exploded into battle when the dragons finally discovered the location of the long-sought flaming jewels. That attack soon led to others, then to wider war, then to madness.

Despite Basilgarrad's heroic efforts, the goal of peace seemed more and more like an elusive mirage. Fireroot's clashes quickly swept up other peoples. Losses mounted, bitterness grew, and rage erupted everywhere. Alliances formed, pitting the dwarves, most elves and humans, giants from the

high peaks, and many clans of eaglefolk against the fire dragons' cohorts—the industrious but warlike flamelons, dark
elves, gnomes, greedy humans, and hordes of gobsken. Even
some clans of faeries, among the most peaceful creatures in
Avalon, joined in the fighting when dragons set fire to their
forest homes. As the fighting spread, reaching well beyond
Fireroot, marauding bands of ogres and angry mountain trolls
took full advantage of the chaos, pillaging villages and crop-
lands wherever they chose.

The War of Storms, as it came to be called, spread to every
realm, making Basilgarrad fly around constantly. Despite the
growing horrors around him, he tried his best—ending a battle before it destroyed a beautiful valley, dispersing a band of
ogres, smashing the weapons of flamelons, and rescuing a village set ablaze by dragons. But for every success, there seemed
to be a dozen failures—more battles, more ogres, more weapons, and more blazes than he could possibly control. A few
brave souls helped him, sometimes at the cost of their lives.
Others did their part—such as Bendegeit, highlord of the
water dragons, who resisted every effort by the fire dragons
to form an alliance. For the most part, however, Basilgarrad
carried the burden of peacemaking on his shoulders alone.

Broad shoulders they were—immensely broad. He was
indisputably the most powerful being who had ever lived in
Avalon. Yet in the midst of this rampant chaos, he sometimes
felt as weak as a newborn faery.

"Merlin!" he bellowed one night to the sky and stars. He

lay, sprawled with exhaustion, on Mudroot's plains of Isenwy. After a long string of battles, he'd landed here, hoping to get some much-needed rest. Yet even though the land around him seemed tranquil, for a change, his mind exploded with thoughts about this terrible war and what it meant for Avalon. And also about that particular person he missed more than ever.

"Where are you in all this catastrophe?" he roared, pounding his titanic tail on the muddy flats, causing tremors for leagues around. "The world needs you. The people need you. And, Merlin . . . *I* need you."

No answer came. Not that he'd expected to hear one. Yet he had, at some level, still hoped. Was Merlin right that the wicked shadow beast could be somewhere far away from Avalon? Or was that merely an excuse for him to depart, a reason to leave this world that had brought him so much pain?

He scanned the darkened sky. When his gaze came to rest on the empty black gash that was once the luminous Wizard's Staff, he grimaced, gnashing his rows of teeth together. And he thought about the wizard's parting words: *I will be with you—for as long as the stars shine bright over Avalon.*

Glumly, Basilgarrad lowered his massive head, until it squelched down in the mud. *That beast is somewhere right here in Avalon. I can feel it! But where? And just what is it, really? What are its powers? Its plans?*

Wrestling with these questions, he eventually fell into a

troubled, uneasy sleep. Yet his dreams, at least, gave him a small measure of escape. He dreamed about his youth in the forests of Woodroot—when all he needed to worry about was how to survive another day without getting eaten by somebody else.

29: LAUGHTER

*One thing I've noticed about living: Once you start doing it,
the habit forms and it's awfully hard to stop.*

The creatures of the Haunted Marsh kept moving away from
the pit of death. Incessantly, in the darkness, they struggled
to escape from that wicked place. Whether they slithered, like
the maggots and worms, or crawled, like the unseen beasts who
dined on rotting flesh, or floated, like the marsh ghouls—they
migrated away from the pit as fast as possible. In time, all that
remained were the rotting corpses that had been there for
ages . . . and the beast everyone else wanted desperately to
avoid.

Doomraga, already enormous, continued to swell. And
swell. And swell. Now its immense, writhing body bulged to
the point of bursting, smashing against the walls of the pit,
crushing anything it touched.

Yet the beast kept expanding. The shadow leech grew
steadily, little by little, hour by hour. Under its swelling skin,
strange ripples began to move, like ominous currents flowing
in a darkened sea. With those ripples came a low, gurgling

sound, as if something poisonous bubbled just beneath the surface.

Another sound, even more terrible, often joined that one. Doomraga's laugh, a raspy, bone-chilling noise, echoed across the dark reaches of the marsh with increasing frequency. For deep in its dark heart, the leech felt a new and pleasing sensation—not true happiness, but a growing sense of anticipation.

Of victory over its enemies, the accursed foes of Rhita Gawr. Of conquest. And, together with its master in the Otherworld, of dominance over Avalon.

Two changes caused this anticipation. First, just as Doomraga had planned, chaos and panic and hatred were spreading swiftly across the realms of this world. The shadow beast sensed all that negative energy, smelled it on the air. Even without the messages from its minions, of whom five or six still survived, Doomraga knew that terror now ruled the land. All the better!

Second, that meddling wizard Merlin had finally departed. Where he had gone and why, Doomraga didn't know. But the fact that Avalon's wizard was gone could not be disputed. That left only one mortal creature—that hated green dragon—who stood in the way.

Doomraga's laughter shook the marsh, touching everything like a deadly wind. For it knew that the dragon's meager efforts were about to end—just as much more was about to end. The time had almost arrived when Avalon would experience Doomraga's greatest feat, its master stroke, its ultimate weapon. At last! Nothing could possibly deter this new force . . . certainly not a simpleminded dragon.

The dreadful laughter exploded again, reaching farther than ever, seeping beyond the borders of the Haunted Marsh. An ancient elm, growing in the rocky soil outside the marsh, suddenly shuddered. Leaves shriveled, roots constricted, and the tree's burly branches started to wither.

Even so, the old elm didn't collapse. As Doomraga's laughter faded away, the tree's roots pushed deeper into the ground and its branches reached again for the sky. Leaves regained their color; heartwood quivered with new life. Such resilience might have surprised Doomraga, who was already savoring the taste of victory. But there was something important that it didn't fully comprehend.

Despite all the leech's plans, and despite all of Avalon's troubles, that tree—like its world—was not yet ready to die.

30: FIRE FROM ABOVE

The beauty and tragedy of a spring day comes from the same simple fact: It's always so brief.

The fire dragons gave no warning.

On a warm day in spring, when the first apple blossoms had just appeared, the dragons descended on the sacred compound of the Society of the Whole in Stoneroot, dropping out of the sky like blazing balls of fire. Within moments, smoke curled upward from burning buildings and screams pierced the stillness of surrounding farms that normally never heard any sounds louder than a ringing bell.

Priestesses and priests—along with their loyal maryths, creatures of all descriptions who joined them in a lifelong bond—worked feverishly to drag the wounded or dazed to safety. But nowhere was safe for long. The air buzzed with panicking mist faeries, pigeons, and barn swallows. Frightened goats, horses, and chickens dashed around the compound, crashing into fleeing people, shrieking and bleating, squawking and whinnying. Children ran everywhere, too scared even to hide in the barns, tool sheds, or limeberry bushes.

Rhia, carrying Nuic on her shoulder, dashed to the enormous Buckle Bell. Heaving on the rope, she made the great bell chime seven times, then stop, then chime seven more times—the Society's distress signal. Before the final echoes began to fade, she ran off to help others, dodging blasts of flame from the circling dragons. She tore one of the vines off the sleeve of her suit to bandage a young goat's singed leg. Then she joined Lleu in tying ropes to keep a burning tree from toppling onto the pillars of the Great Temple. Moments later, she started hurling buckets of water onto the flames that raged on the roof of the library.

Yet all this wasn't enough. As Nuic's darkening gray color indicated, the compound and its neighboring farms would soon be destroyed, swallowed by flames and panic.

Leagues away, a family of mountain giants was crossing the plains. Led by the fearsome Jubolda—known across the realm for lifting off the tops of hills to expose the caves of marauding trolls—each of their strides was the size of a farmer's field. Suddenly they heard the Buckle Bell's call of distress. Immediately, Jubolda and her three gargantuan daughters turned and strode in the direction of the compound. On the way, they were joined by another giant who had also heard the bell: none other than Shim.

"I surely hopes we arrives in time to save those nicely people," he muttered, his huge feet slamming against the ground.

"Not me," answered Jubolda. Her earrings, made of waterwheels from an abandoned granary, jostled with each of her steps. "I want to arrive in time to demolish whoever dared attack the Society! Fire dragons, from that smell of smoke in the air."

Shim glanced over at her. With a rub of his bulbous nose, he said, "Just be careful, Lady Jubolda. You is a giantess, but you is still mortally mortal. We don't want you getting hurted by them dragons."

Jubolda merely waved away his concern. But one of her daughters—whose enormous, drooling lips had inspired the name Bonlog Mountain-Mouth—looked at Shim with grateful adoration.

The giants arrived not a moment too soon. Fire dragons were attacking the largest building in the compound, a structure made entirely of countless branches broken by winter storms. No building could be more flammable. Or more cherished. Its high, peaked archways rose like pinnacles; its stained glass windows shone with the radiance of bright-winged butterflies. And in that building, called the Crafts Community, generations of priestesses and priests had learned the skills of pottery, weaving, basketry, glass blowing, and woodworking. Even Pwyll Estonna, the most famous sculptor of the artisan elves, discovered her gifts within its walls. To see that old house go up in flames would have broken the hearts of everyone who knew it.

Three dragons swooped down from the sky, their scarlet wings as bright as flames. Simultaneously, they roared, sending fiery blasts straight at the building's roof. At that very instant, three gigantic hands reached out and blocked the fire from reaching its target. Those hands, belonging to Jubolda,

Shim, and Bonlog, immediately closed into immense fists that slammed full-force into the attackers.

Explosions shook the air as the giants' knuckles smashed into the dragons' scaly chests, sending them into a tailspin. They crashed, ribs and tails broken, in a nearby pasture. For them, the battle was abruptly over; crawling away from the giants was now their only goal.

The remaining fire dragons, eight or nine in number, quickly changed tactics. Like angry hornets, they ferociously attacked the giants, ripping at them with terrible claws and shooting blasts of flame. Even so, they proved to be no match for their foes, whose thickly calloused skin shielded better than armor. Jubolda lost one of her earrings (which only made her more angry), but none of her companions suffered worse than minor scratches. The fire dragons fared much worse. Several of them fell to the giants' flying fists, while one unlucky dragon perished in the teeth of Bonlog Mountain-Mouth.

Rhia, helping douse the flames on the crafts building roof, cheered this turn of fortune. Hope swelled in her heart that the terrors of this day, which had started as such a fragrant spring morning, would soon end. Then, looking to the east, she saw something so startling that she dropped her water bucket.

Flamelon warriors! Marching in rigid formation, the soldiers from Fireroot started to encircle the compound. Wheeling into place heavy iron catapults, made in their volcanic forges, they fired deadly volleys at the giants. Immense boulders slammed into the huge beings' chests and arms. Vats of boiling oil burst upon their backs. Nets made of sturdy rope tangled their powerful legs, making them stumble.

Sensing their improved chances, the fire dragons pressed their attack. All around the compound, towers of smoke rose into the air, staining the sky. Dragons' tails slashed violently at buildings, walls, and monuments. Wounded men, women, and children ran, shrieking and wailing, in all directions.

Shim, hearing a bellowing howl, turned to see a giant who had fallen to the ground. Bonlog! She flailed helplessly, her legs tangled in a net. Meanwhile, a troop of flamelons marched swiftly toward her, brandishing a terrible array of broadswords and spears.

"Stop!" Though he wasn't sure how to help, Shim started to run toward her—but caught an enormous toe on the compound's outer wall. He pitched forward, falling like a massive tree.

Shouting and waving his arms wildly, he tried to regain his balance. To no avail. He shut his eyes and slammed down to the ground. His huge body struck with such force that a nearby catapult teetered from the vibrations and then collapsed. Shim, knowing that he'd failed to help Bonlog, didn't want to open his eyes lest he see her lifeless body, mutilated by the flamelons.

I is such a failure! he thought. *Such a clumsily failure!*

Someone shoved him—roughly, with the strength of a giant. He opened his eyes. To his astonishment, he was looking up at Bonlog!

"You is . . . alive?" he asked.

She opened her gargantuan mouth in a smile. "Thanks to you, Shim! You saved me—by throwing your body on top of those flamelons."

Blinking with surprise, he rolled over. Sure enough, the crushed remains of the entire troop lay beneath him. "But . . . but I—" he stammered.

"That was so brave of you, Shim. So bold. So . . ." She paused, her eyes glittering, as she wiped a foamy river of spit off her chin. "So *masculine*."

Shim's mood swiftly changed from surprise to panic. That feeling spread as he saw, to his horror, Bonlog Mountain-Mouth bending down to give him a kiss. Her gigantic, saliva-drenched lips drew closer. Rivers of spit gushed from the cavernous depths of her mouth. Her puckering lips swelled, obscuring half her face.

"Eeeek!" cried Shim. With amazing speed, he rolled aside, bounced to his feet, and sped away, running as fast as he could toward the safety of the high peaks.

The giantess stood again, scowling as she watched him escape. From the depths of her throat came an angry curse, then a giant-size sigh of disappointment. Reluctantly, she rejoined the fight against the fire dragons and flamelons, battling alongside her mother. Yet every few seconds, she paused to look longingly at the departing figure she could still see on the horizon. As Shim finally vanished from view, she breathed another great sigh, spraying a lake's worth of spit. Glumly, she wiped her cavernous mouth and stepped back into the fray.

Even with Bonlog back in action, the battle went badly for the defenders. Building by building, the dragons set fire to the compound, leaving the survivors few places to hide. The flamelons pressed closer, tightening their deadly noose. Although Rhia continued to shout encouragement to her followers, she didn't believe her own words.

All they had done to build this place, to honor the highest ideals of Avalon and their dreams of what it could become— all this was lost forever. She knew it. Nuic, clinging to her shoulder, was now pitch-black.

"Look!" cried Lleu. He pointed his bloodstained arm toward the sky.

Rhia looked up to see another dragon, swiftly approaching. But this was no fire dragon. This was a dragon whose bright green scales, massive wings, and powerful tail could not be mistaken.

"Basil!" she cried. "It's Basilgarrad!"

At the mere sound of his name, several fire dragons shrieked and fled. Those who hesitated soon regretted their mistake. The moment he reached the compound, his clubbed tail slammed into one dragon, hurling its body all the way to the southern marshes. An instant later, he spun around and struck another hard enough to break every rib in its chest. Before that attacker even hit the ground, he looped his great tail around another's neck and threw it somewhere beyond the edge of the realm. Meanwhile, he butted his head against the back of another's skull—so forcefully that one of its eyes flew out, landing in a lake several leagues away.

Seeing this mighty display of force, the flamelons blew their horns and hastily retreated. Skilled warriors that they were, they knew they couldn't prevail against such an overwhelmingly superior foe. Yet some of their commanders hung back, studying Basilgarrad for any signs of weakness. For they knew, beyond doubt, that they would fight this dragon again. And when that happened, they did not intend to be defeated.

In time, the smoky skies cleared. It took many months of labor, but Rhia and her surviving followers cremated their lost loved ones, rebuilt the damaged buildings, and restored the gardens of the compound. The Great Temple's pillars were repaired, and most of the scorches cleaned. Priestesses and priests and their maryths rejoiced when, once again, the Buckle Bell rang—this time not in distress, but in welcome. To all those in Avalon who still valued peace. Even the scattered faeries returned, their wings glowing with the colors of blue sky, rosy blossoms, and silver mist.

Yet no one could ever forget the dreadful day that came to be called the Battle of the Withered Spring. Nor the great green dragon who had finally prevailed.

31: THE DARK GASH

Whoever said "It's always darkest before the dawn" clearly wasn't with me on that long night.

One night, Basilgarrad lay alone on the rim of Prism Gorge in the upper reaches of Waterroot. He couldn't sleep. His tail, stretched along the multicolored ledge, gleamed with red, yellow, and purple dust that shone in the starlight as he turned and tossed.

That very day, he'd heard from a passing sylph that the fire dragons were massing for yet another attack on Woodroot. So far, he'd prevented them from burning many of its trees, but how much longer could he prevail? The sylph warned, too, that they had tried to form an alliance with Bendegeit's water dragons—and that, when the highlord refused, they incited a rebellion against him. Led by the royal guard called Scarface, whom Basilgarrad had so enjoyed outwitting, the rebellion had failed. Bendegeit triumphed, preserving his rule. But there was no guarantee that there wouldn't be another uprising in the future—with a different result.

And what about Marnya? Had she survived the rebellion? Basilgarrad's whole body shuddered, sending up a cloud of multicolored dust from the ledge. This night's perch by the gorge was the closest he'd come, since his visit to Bendegeit's lair, to her home in the Rainbow Seas. In the time since then, he'd thought about her often—more often than he wanted to admit. He'd heard that she continued to practice her new-found skill at flying, and was often seen soaring through those misty skies. For some time he'd wanted to visit her, but his unending work made that impossible.

Why am I thinking about her? he asked himself with an annoyed rumble. *I should be sleeping while I can.*

Yet even as he asked the question, he knew the answer. Something in that dragon's luminous blue eyes and adventurous spirit, something in the way she roared with delight when he'd carried her into the air, had touched him more deeply than he'd expected.

Forget about it, he told himself grumpily. *You have too much work to do!*

Work. That was all he ever did! The more Avalon's troubles multiplied, the more he rushed from realm to realm, trying to stop the latest outrage. With what success? Not much, really. While he'd managed to stem a great deal of violence and destruction, the bitter truth could not be denied. Avalon was dying! No matter how much he did, the scale of its problems only worsened.

I must, he realized, *try something different. Drastically different. But what?*

Raising his massive tail, he slammed it down on the rocky rim. Dust of every hue rose into the air, obscuring the stars, as boulders broke off and clattered down into the gorge. *It is time*, he vowed with sudden inspiration, *to find Merlin! To convince him to come home.*

How, though? Basilgarrad himself couldn't do it. If he left Avalon for just a few days—or even a few minutes, the way things were going—the realms would surely descend into chaos. Whatever that shadow beast really was, whatever powers it served, would then triumph. And the journey to find Merlin would certainly take more than a few days.

He lifted his enormous face toward the starry sky. One of those lights, perhaps, was the world called Earth. And the pathway there required climbing all the way up the Great Tree, out to the farthest tip of the highest branch—and beyond. Who could possibly do that?

Rhia, he knew, was the perfect choice. She possessed all the right qualities—bravery, boldness, wisdom, and that persuasive skill that came from being Merlin's sister. Basilgarrad blew a heavy sigh, causing a dust storm on the gorge's rim. For he knew, after his last visit with Rhia, that she wouldn't be available. For anything. He frowned, recalling their conversation outside the rebuilt walls of her compound.

"I've made a decision, Basil," she had declared. She peered up at him and shook her head, making her silvery curls bounce against her shoulders. "A decision to"—she paused, tightening her jaw—"to leave."

"Leave?" roared the dragon in surprise. "For where?"

"I don't know," she replied, deep sadness in her eyes. "I

am only sure that it's time for me to leave this compound, this realm . . . and never come back."

She twisted one of the vines on her sleeve. "All this warfare, all this killing—Basil, it's breaking my heart. And, what is almost as painful, the Society is gripped by fear. Priests and priestesses are growing more rigid, more locked into fundamentalist beliefs, every day. This just isn't the order my mother founded anymore, an order grounded in love and respect for all living creatures."

"But you are the High Priestess!"

She shook her head. "No more."

"You won't reconsider?" he pleaded. "We need you here, Rhia. To fight for Avalon! We can still save it, if we—"

"No," she interrupted. "I just don't have the strength, Basil. Nor the will." She exhaled slowly. "And without those . . . I'm only a burden. That's why I must leave."

And so their conversation had come to an end. Would it be their last? Would they possibly meet again someday in the future? No one could know.

Basilgarrad stirred restlessly on the rim of the gorge. Somberly, he lifted his great head to look at the dark gash in the night sky, the place where a bright row of stars once burned with fierce radiance. The Wizard's Staff. Where had those stars gone? What had caused them to go dark? What role did that vanished constellation play in the elusive puzzle of Avalon's fate—the puzzle that had tormented him for so long?

All these questions, he knew, only Merlin could answer. Just as he knew that there was only one person left in all of Avalon who might be able to make the journey to find the wizard. The very last person Basilgarrad wanted to ask. The very last person who would agree to help.

The dragon, still gazing at the empty spot in the sky, ground his teeth together. Difficult as it would be, he needed to try. Tomorrow, he would fly to Krystallus.

32: MAGICAL MAPS

There are many ways of being lost. In some cases, no map can help.

Where, wondered Basilgarrad, should he look for Krystallus? The best place to start was the center for exploration he'd founded—the Eopia College of Mapmakers. Located by a powerful portal at the easternmost tip of Brynchilla, the college now boasted the largest collection of maps in Avalon. Its well-traveled residents made regular journeys to the seven root-realms, and also (rumor had it) to the misty shores of Lost Fincayra in the spirit realm.

Many people lived at the college, whether to learn the craft of mapmaking or to record their newest discoveries. Among them was Krystallus. He had traveled much farther than anyone else—including, on a recent journey, a secret route into the very trunk of the Tree, to an interior cavern he named the Great Hall of the Heartwood. Yet that discovery, like all the rest he'd made in his storied career, only increased his appetite for more.

Basilgarrad swooped out of the clouds, catching his first glimpse of the college. *What sort of building is that?* he wondered, peering down at a colorful patchwork of old blankets, faded tunics, and ground cloths beside a sheer cliff. Some pieces of fabric shone with glittering, magical threads; others took most of their color from the dirt of their travels.

Puzzled, he glided lower. As the angular shadow of his wing passed over the college, he suddenly understood. *It's a tent! A gigantic tent.* Either Krystallus, in building the college, wanted to evoke the itinerant life of an explorer who often slept in a tent or on open ground, or he simply hadn't found enough time to construct something sturdier.

Basilgarrad landed beside the huge enclosure, skidding on the loose rocks atop the cliff. He ambled closer, dragging his enormous tail behind him, taking care not to disturb an outdoor lecture by some woman in a hair shirt who was describing her adventures in Trolldom. Engrossed by her talk (and by the tame one-eyed troll who stood by her side, trying to catch passing birds on its tongue), her audience gave only fleeting attention to Basilgarrad. He was, after all, a familiar sight around Avalon, whereas a troll was something truly exotic. As the dragon passed by, the audience gasped when the troll shot out its tongue and nabbed an unlucky seagull.

Approaching the tent's open wall, which had been rolled up to make a wide entryway, Basilgarrad laid his enormous head on the ground outside. People continued to bustle in and out of the tent, walking around his snout with barely a glance at him, as if there was nothing at all strange about finding a dragon on the college grounds. Some of them were deep in conversation about faraway places, such as the two young men in feathered hats who were arguing over the nature of Airroot's cloudcake. Others were carrying heaps of scrolls, piled so high in their arms that spills happened frequently. Still others chattered or sang in languages that even Basilgarrad, with all his travels, had never heard.

This place feels more like a circus than a college, he thought, watching a team of dwarves lead a wide-eared elephaunt into the tent.

His curiosity piqued, he peered inside. Hanging from the top of the tent was a huge blue banner with the emblem he knew well: a star within a circle, the ancient symbol for travel between places and times. Directly beneath it stood something that made him snort in surprise—a scale model of the Great Tree of Avalon, rotating slowly on its stand. Wondrously detailed in its representations of the seven root-realms, the model tree showed forests, lakes, marshes, settlements, and landmarks of all kinds. Descriptive labels dotted its surface. But its branches, as yet unexplored, showed hardly any features at all.

"Excuse me, master dragon."

Basilgarrad lowered his gaze to see a young elf standing beside his jaw. Though taller than most elves, his head barely reached the dragon's lower lip. "Yes?" the great voice rumbled.

"Aren't you Wings of Peace?" asked the elf, his forest green eyes looking up into a much larger eye of similar shade.

"I am," answered the immensely deep voice. "Although these days, peace is hard to find."

The elf nodded. Apparently more interested in the past than the present, he asked, "Is it true you hatched from your egg at the very moment of Avalon's birth?" Wrinkling his brow, he added, "Though you really didn't take your dragon's form until later—when you were thirty-seven years old, to be precise."

The corners of Basilgarrad's mouth curled in a smile. "Yes, that's true. And you, I would guess, must be Tressimir—the young historian among the wood elves."

Blushing, the elf asked, "You have heard of me?"

"Dragons have big ears." He gave a rumbling chuckle. "Now tell me, Tressimir, do you have any idea where I might find Krystallus?"

The elf brightened. "Why, yes! He was here just this morning, working on that new map idea. You know, the one that can—"

"I don't know," interrupted Basilgarrad. "But could you find him for me?"

"Of course." Tressimir hurried into the tent, joining the throng of people inside.

Watching him, Basilgarrad decided to take a closer look at what was going on in there. Along one wall, he saw several partitions that created smaller spaces. *Classrooms*, he realized. Within each space, someone was lecturing to a group of listeners. To illustrate their points, the lecturers often broke into chants, songs, or wild cries. At other times, they held up drawings, sample pieces of clothing, plaster casts of footprints, or (in one case) an enormous gold-colored claw.

Against the wall at the far side of the tent, behind the model of the Tree, dozens of students sat at individual desks. Each held an eagle quill pen in one hand and a rough sketch map in the other, while drawing on the paper scroll spread upon the desk. Ink bottles, more quills, blotting cloths, and compasses lay strewn everywhere.

A noble craft, thought the dragon approvingly. *It takes a lot of skill to draw a decent map.*

Nudging a bit closer to the entrance, he realized that all around the floor were displays of other kinds of maps—some that he'd heard rumors about, and others that he'd never have dreamed possible. There, beside the rotating Tree, was an upright stand holding a large map that could actually talk! Famous for its deep baritone voice—as well as its propensity to start whistling at any given moment—it had been a gift to the college from Krystallus. But he had never revealed exactly where he'd found it. Bards from every realm came here to stand before that map and ask questions about faraway lands. Right now, a group of woodland faeries were fluttering about it, asking where they might live without any danger of battles, fires, or explosions.

Basilgarrad's ears stretched forward, as he listened with great interest for the answer. But to his dismay—and the faeries' outrage—the map remained silent. It would not speak, nor even whistle. The faeries, in a huff, buzzed off angrily, nearly flying into Basilgarrad's nose as they left the tent.

Just as I suspected, he thought somberly. *Which is why we need to bring back Merlin.*

He scanned the bustling tent again, looking for any sign of Krystallus. Finding none, he turned back to the unusual maps on display. First to catch his eye—or, more accurately, his ear—was the Map of Songs. Donated to the college by a family of museos, it could produce the local music of any place in Avalon. Just now, an elf maiden was pressing her finger against the very tip of Airroot. Instantly, the map burst into the swishing, windy music sung by sylphs who floated among the clouds.

Gazing around the tent, Basilgarrad spotted another map, one that could do the work of a telescope. With the proper incantation, it could give people a close-up view of anywhere on the landscape. Thirty or forty people were standing in line, awaiting a turn—including a bent old woman with gnarled hair, arms like knotted branches, and feet the shape of tree roots.

A treeling, the dragon realized. *I thought there were none of them left.*

Intrigued though he was, his attention turned to another map, this one in the form of a dimly lit sphere. Made from some kind of crystal, it swirled with shadowy gases, as if it contained a small but magical storm. Basilgarrad frowned, wrinkling his massive brow, for it reminded him of the magical sphere of Bendegeit—and the dark apparition he'd seen within it.

Just then a woman, wearing a heavy shawl over her hunched shoulders, approached the sphere. "Tell me," she demanded in a raspy voice, "what will my home look like in two hundred years?"

A map that shows the future! Basilgarrad slid forward a bit more, eager to hear what place the woman had in mind. And how it would look after two more centuries. He shuddered, suddenly wondering if *any* of Avalon would be left after that much time, given all the destruction of the war.

"My home," the woman rasped, "is found on the westernmost point of Lastrael—in a new settlement my people are building. It will take longer to finish than I have years left to live, but I want to know what it will look like."

Lastrael? That's Shadowroot. Always dark, always dangerous. Why would anyone settle there? Basilgarrad scrunched his nose in sympathy. *Poor old woman, she won't see anything but darkness.*

Within the sphere, shadows swirled. The scene grew steadily darker, until there was nothing but inky blackness. It was a scene befitting the realm of endless night.

Abruptly—the whole globe radiated light. Fires blazed everywhere in a coastal city—a city made of light more than anything solid. The woman, her face aglow from the sphere, nodded in approval.

Basilgarrad caught his breath. *A city of light?* He peered more closely at the old woman. *Who is she?*

While he didn't recognize her, he did detect a smoky, smoldering smell as she came nearer. Then he noticed something new about her heavy shawl—a pair of bumps that didn't seem like shoulders. Could they, perhaps, be the upper edges of wings?

He was about to ask her who she really was and where she

came from, when someone tapped the base of his jaw. "Well, well," said a deep voice. "What in Dagda's name brings you here?"

Reluctantly, Basilgarrad pulled his gaze from the old woman, who was now leaving the tent—and trained it on the man who had spoken. "Hello, Krystallus."

33: WHILE THIS WORLD STILL LASTS

I like secrets, and always have. But only when I know them.

The rugged-looking man, whose long white hair brushed his sturdy shoulders, nodded in greeting. "Nice to see you, Basil. Did you come to view one of our magical maps?" Before the dragon could respond, he lifted a purple vial into the air. "This new one, perhaps? It's only just been bottled after eighteen days of magical distilling—a little trick I picked up on my travels."

"Well . . ." began Basilgarrad. He hesitated, wanting to be sure Krystallus was in a good mood before raising the delicate subject of his father. "What exactly is in that vial?"

"Ah!" replied the explorer jubilantly. "Just what I hoped you would ask." He glanced over his shoulder at the young elf Tressimir, who had come back to see more of Basilgarrad. "Could you fetch a tray or a bowl, my good lad? I need something that can hold liquid."

Tressimir reached into the weathered leather satchel that hung from his shoulder. Pulling out a rough wooden bowl, he asked, "Will this do?"

"Perfectly." Krystallus stepped closer to the dragon, so

that he wasn't in the path of all the people entering and leaving the tent. At the same time, Tressimir joined him and handed him the bowl.

"I don't understand," said the dragon, "what that vial has to do with a map."

"Just watch." In one swift motion, Krystallus uncorked the vial and poured its contents into the bowl. As the purple stream gurgled out of the container, he commanded, "Rainbow Seas."

To the astonishment of Basilgarrad as well as Tressimir, the liquid in the bottom of the bowl turned crystal clear and then filled with lines—black ones marking the shapes of islands and coastlines, and silver ones marking altitudes on the land and depths in the water.

"Why," exclaimed the dragon, "it *is* a map! A liquid map."

"Of the Rainbow Seas," added Tressimir. "Look, there is the castle of Queen Serella."

"Yes," said Krystallus with the hint of a grin. "I know it well."

"Impressive." Basilgarrad's attention had moved to another spot on the map—a sheer coastline pocked with caverns, one of which was labeled *Lair of the Highlord of the Water Dragons.* He couldn't help but imagine, rising out of the water by the cavern, the head of a dragon with azure blue eyes.

"Glad you approve," said Krystallus, beaming. Tilting the bowl very carefully, he poured the liquid map back into its vial. "Could be very useful for underwater explorations."

"Underwater?"

"Why, yes, Basil. It's the next frontier." He gestured at the rotating model of the Great Tree in the center of the tent. "After I find a way to explore the branches, that is. And, of course—"

"The stars." Basilgarrad winked at him. "I'm glad you haven't lost sight of that goal."

"Lost sight? I've never stopped thinking about it!" Krystallus pulled the special starward compass from his tunic pocket and gazed at it with longing. Its globe seemed to shine with its own radiance, like a distant star.

After a few seconds, he waved his hand toward a star chart hanging from one of the tent walls. "You see that map of constellations? Every night when I'm here, I study it. Every night. Just in case it will give me some new idea of how to get up there."

Basilgarrad, however, wasn't listening. He was focused on the dark swath on the map where a long-cherished constellation had disappeared. "Krystallus, I must—"

"And over there," continued the explorer, bubbling with enthusiasm, "is a precious treasure—a map of another world." He pointed to a round globe, mostly blue, with oddly shaped continents painted between wide oceans. "Strange, isn't it, to see a world that is completely round, instead of being shaped like a tree! It was a gift from my Aunt Rhia before she left, something she'd been given by her brother."

"Your father."

Basilgarrad's words brought him to an abrupt halt. His

expression hardened; all the enthusiasm melted away. "I don't want to speak about him."

The dragon's enormous eyes widened even more. "Krystallus, we *must* speak about him."

He folded his arms across his chest. "Is that why you came here?"

"Yes. It is." Basilgarrad's ears swiveled. "We need him, Krystallus. We need him back here! You may not know how badly this war is going, with all your travels. It's worse than ever! I can't stop it alone—and believe me, I've been trying. I need Merlin's help to prevail. So, Krystallus . . . you must find him. Before it's too late."

The explorer shook his head slowly, making his white hair rustle. "That's *your* problem, Basil. Not mine."

"No!" bellowed the dragon, so loud that all the activity in and around the tent suddenly ceased. People stopped talking, studying, and admiring the assorted maps, turning their heads to see what was happening. But Basilgarrad paid no attention. He remained entirely focused on Krystallus.

Sliding forward to bring his face right up to the man's, he said in a low rumble, "This is *Avalon's* problem. Not just mine, not just yours. Avalon's. Everyone who lives in this world, from the littlest bubblefish to the biggest dragon, has a stake in the outcome."

Krystallus said nothing.

"We need your help. Avalon needs your help."

The explorer scowled. "He left by his own choice."

"Yes, after you spoke to him the way you did. After that,

he knew he had lost both you and your mother. With so much loss, so much pain, how could he ever stay?"

Although the words made him wince, Krystallus continued to scowl. "No, Basil. I'm not going to chase after him like a young puppy."

The green eyes narrowed. "So your pride is more important than Avalon's survival?"

"I told you, *I'm not going.*"

Basilgarrad tilted his huge head, causing the tip of one ear to push against the side of the tent. "Think of it not as a voyage to find your father. Think of it, instead, as an exploration. As your chance to voyage to the stars! And to a world beyond, the world called Earth."

For the first time, the explorer's face softened slightly. Put in that way, the notion seemed to intrigue him. Then his jaw tightened, and he declared, "No. I am not the person to find him."

"You are the *only* person," the dragon replied.

"Not true, Basil." Krystallus looked up at him with complete certainty. "You could go after him! You could find him."

Basilgarrad's great brow furrowed. "If I do that, this whole world of ours will fall to pieces! You really have no idea, do you? I am rushing from one crisis to the next, every day, all the time, without end."

Deep in his dragon's throat, he growled. "Something is behind all this, Krystallus. Something wholly evil. And it's hiding somewhere here in Avalon! I'm more and more convinced of that. If I leave, even briefly, it will prevail. If I stay, I might prevent that from happening—at least until Merlin returns."

The explorer pursed his lips, still not convinced. "At least, if you go, he might listen to you. But if it's me"—he stopped, clearing his throat—"he wouldn't listen."

The dragon, looking dismayed, opened his jagged wings slightly then tucked them against his back. "I must go now, Krystallus. I heard only yesterday that the fire dragons are massing to attack Woodroot."

"El Urien!" exclaimed Tressimir, his forest-colored eyes alight. "They could set the whole realm on fire!"

"That's their goal, I'm sure. But I plan to stop them. And I will have help. Already, many of Woodroot's bravest residents are gathering at the headwaters of the River Relentless."

The young elf straightened. "Then I should be there, too."

"Tressimir, are you sure?" asked Krystallus. "What about that history of the college you are writing?"

"That will have to wait." The elf looked at him squarely. "By the great goddess Lorilanda, this is my home we are talking about! A land whose every tree I know by name. I must do whatever I can to protect it."

Above him, the dragon's head bobbed. "So must we all."

Grimly, Krystallus glanced from one to the other. Placing his hands on Tressimir's shoulders, he said, "All right, then. But keep yourself safe. You already have more knowledge in your young head than I have in all my maps."

Lowering his hands, he stepped closer to the elf. "Here. Take this with you. It's something valuable—so valuable I keep it with me always. But now"—he reached into a pocket in the neck of his tunic and pulled out a small, folded piece of parchment—"I give it to you."

Krystallus slid the parchment into Tressimir's satchel. Then, leaning forward, he whispered something into the elf's ear. As he spoke, Tressimir's eyebrows lifted in surprise.

As Krystallus finished, the elf asked, "Are you sure?"

"Yes, lad, I am sure. Just remember what I told you." He shot a quick glance at the dragon, who was watching them quizzically. "When the time is right."

"The time is right for me to leave," declared Basilgarrad. "Krystallus, are you sure about your decision?"

"I am."

"Then I leave you to your explorations—while this world still lasts."

Krystallus bristled, but didn't answer.

"And you, Tressimir. Would you like to have a ride to Woodroot?"

"Of course!" As the dragon lowered his ear to the ground, the elf eagerly scampered up.

Basilgarrad and Krystallus peered at each other for several seconds. Then, without another word, the dragon backed away from the great patchwork tent, opened his wide wings, and leaped into the sky. He circled once, gaining altitude with every stroke, then vanished into the clouds.

The explorer's sharp eyes followed, watching the sky even after they disappeared. In a voice so quiet that only he could hear, Krystallus repeated the dragon's parting words: "while this world still lasts."

Finally, he turned and strode into the tent.

34: THE GREAT BATTLE

I never mind a battle to the death—as long as I'm nowhere near it.

Wind rushed past Basilgarrad's face as he flew rapidly to Woodroot, carrying the elf Tressimir atop his head. Light flashed on the green scales of his snout, wings, and back, as if they had been polished by the scouring wind. Despite all the stress he'd felt since Avalon's cauldron of turmoil boiled over into war, his wings felt sturdy and strong. They propelled him through the air, throwing his body forward with every downstroke, a living embodiment of grace and power.

Yet he wasn't enjoying this flight. All he could think about was Avalon's desperate need for Merlin—and his son's refusal to help. *That foolish Krystallus! He's as stubborn as . . .* The dragon hesitated, searching for the right words. *As his father.*

Tressimir, for his part, was relishing the experience. Wrapping an arm around the dragon's upright ear, he leaned forward, feeling the wind buffet his face and flap the sleeves of his tunic. His satchel blew straight behind him, straining at its strap, but the elf was too absorbed in this new adventure to notice. He studied the lands, rivers, canyons, and misty corridors below, trying to memorize their locations. Even more, he tried to soak in the wondrous feeling of flight—perfectly thrilling, utterly free.

Soon after green forests appeared below, Basilgarrad flew lower, practically skimming the treetops. For Tressimir, this offered a view of his homeland he had never before experienced, allowing him to view it as would a soaring hawk. For Basilgarrad, though, the greatest benefit was not the sights, but the smells. As he glided over the trees, he caught the scents of sweet resins, tart plums, tangy mushrooms, and more. The richness of those smells pulled him out of his worries and gave him a brief but potent reminder of why it was worth fighting to protect his beloved realm.

The dragon veered to follow the winding path of the River Relentless, climbing toward its source. Below, the river tumbled down rocky stretches or poured over falls. The frothing white water shot curtains of spray into the air, rimmed with rainbows. The dragon's shadow seemed to sail up the rapids, moving as fluidly as the water itself.

As they ascended, the river started to narrow, flowing through a tree-lined canyon. In time the canyon's walls lowered, gradually merging into the rolling meadows of the El Urien uplands. The river, meanwhile, diminished in size, becoming a stream and then a thin rivulet. Choosing a wide, flat field, Basilgarrad landed.

"The headwaters," announced Tressimir, amazed at how quickly they had arrived. He marveled at the beauty of these lush meadows, sprinkled with white marigolds, yellow faery crowns, and some bright blue flowers that smelled like cedar cones.

Basilgarrad's attention, by contrast, was not on the landscape—but on the people waiting for them. A band of centaurs, fierce and proud, stood by the rivulet, stamping their hooves impatiently. Men and women, carrying shields and spears and broadswords, had gathered nearby. Most of them gazed at the dragon, while a few continued to sing a woodland harmony. Horses, a few bears, and a herd of white-tailed deer milled around, pausing now and then to drink the clear water. Dozens of eaglefolk circled overhead, their silver wings shining; numerous hawks and falcons, plus at least one immense canyon eagle, flew with them. Far away, marching swiftly, came an enormous band of elves. Even at a distance, the dragon could see their dark green tunics along with their hunting bows and quivers of arrows.

More of them than I expected, thought Basilgarrad, watching grimly. *But will it be enough?*

Just then he caught a faint smell on the air—the odor of charred scales and bloodied claws. *Fire dragons.*

He whirled around, the club of his tail nearly brushing the startled centaurs. But Basilgarrad didn't notice. His attention remained fixed on the dark, distant shapes flying toward them. Gnashing his teeth, he realized that there were over a hundred fire dragons approaching—more than he'd ever been forced to face in battle. His great heart beat faster, as his shoulder muscles tensed.

"What is it?" cried Tressimir, not yet seeing the invaders but feeling the dragon's reaction.

Basilgarrad did not respond, except to lower his ear so the elf could climb down. For he had just glimpsed, on the horizon, another trace of movement. And a new cause for concern.

Flamelons! A vast army of battle-hardened warriors marched toward them. Striding in perfect formation, the army seemed like a single, connected body—an irresistible force that would destroy anything or anyone in its path. Rising out of the lines of warriors were the towers of catapults and flame hurlers, two of the flamelons' most deadly inventions.

Watching them, his heart racing, Basilgarrad noticed another kind of tower in their ranks. Much taller than the catapults, this structure rocked back and forth as the flamelons wheeled it closer. Its base held a wide platform with a large wooden crate. What the crate might hold, he couldn't tell. Yet he knew that he would soon confront a new kind of weapon.

By the breath of Dagda, what is that thing? In some vague, unexplained way, he sensed that this would be the most terrible invention the flamelons had ever produced. And worse—that its primary purpose was to destroy him, Avalon's greatest defender. A deep, echoing rumble arose from his throat.

Tressimir, who had climbed down to the ground, drew an anxious breath as he watched the enemies approaching by air and land. "This will be a horrid battle," he predicted, "the worst one yet." Tapping the dragon's chin, he added, "But we have a chance to prevail . . . thanks to you."

Basilgarrad, hastily working out a battle plan in his mind, gave a loud snort. "We might prevail, Tressimir, but this war will still drag on. More lives will end, more lands will burn. It will not stop."

"How do you know?" the elf demanded. "This could be the great, decisive battle that ends the war!"

"No." His eye, radiant green, studied the elf somberly. "There are more foes at work here than we can see. I know that, Tressimir—with certainty."

The elf frowned. "You mean that foe you mentioned to Krystallus. The one you called *wholly evil*—the cause of all our troubles."

"That's right. And if I only knew where in Avalon it's hiding—I could destroy it! I could finally end this horror and restore the peace." He sighed a gargantuan sigh, forceful enough to bend the grass on distant meadows. "Without Merlin to help me, though, there's no way to find it."

"But there *is*."

The elf spoke so decisively that Basilgarrad's curiosity swelled. "What do you mean?" he demanded, keeping one wary eye on the sky. "Speak quickly! We have only two or three minutes before those dragons reach us."

Tressimir reached into his satchel and pulled out the parchment from Krystallus. He held it, still folded, in his hand. "This is a map—a very special map. He told me to give it to you so you could find Merlin."

"It's a map to Earth?"

"No! Far better." A wind swept across the meadow, making the parchment quiver. "It's a map to *any place you want to go*. Any place at all. On this world or any other."

The dragon's tail thumped the ground excitedly, upsetting many of the deer and horses. "No wonder Krystallus considered it so valuable!"

Tressimir nodded. "He won it in a wager with Domnu, the old hag from Fincayra. And he's been guarding it ever since, planning to use it someday on his voyage to the stars."

"Yet he parted with it to help Avalon." The dragon's eyes glinted. "So like his father."

Pausing to scowl at the approaching fire dragons, Basilgarrad declared, "After I defeat these invaders, I'll use the map to find Merlin! With its help, I can do that much faster than I ever thought possible—and fast enough, let's hope, that Avalon's enemies won't cause too much damage. Then Merlin and I can use the map to locate—and destroy—that evil beast! And when all that is done, I'll return the map to Krystallus so he can use it on his voyage."

The elf bit his lip. "No, you won't."

"Why not?"

"Because . . . this map can be used only once."

The dragon stared down at him. "Once?"

"Alas," said Tressimir, "that is the limit of its magic. Which means—"

"I must make a choice."

"A terrible choice. Either you use it to find Merlin—or the beast. But not both." Tressimir shook his head. The wind surged again, smelling strongly of charred dragons' scales. "You should decide later, when you have enough time to think everything through."

"No!" roared the dragon, his nostrils flaring. "I have already decided. I will use the map to show me where to find the beast." Nudging the elf with his nose, he added, "And I want to do it *now*."

"Now? But the fire dragons . . . the battle . . ."

"Will begin in seconds, I know! But Tressimir, anything could happen in the fighting. The map could be lost or destroyed. Let's use it while we have this moment. Right now!"

"All right, then." Carefully opening the map, Tressimir quickly explained, "Train your thoughts on what you want to find. Then say the words 'show me the way.'"

Basilgarrad peered at the small, brittle piece of parchment. Totally blank except for a small drawing of a circular compass in the upper left corner, it gave no indication that it held any magic. Let alone magic of such power.

This must work, he thought passionately. *For Avalon's sake.* Gathering all his energy, he focused his mind on the shadowy beast he'd glimpsed in Bendegeit's sphere—the beast who was behind all this turmoil.

His deep voice bellowed, "Show me the way."

Nothing happened. One second passed. Then another. Then another. Basilgarrad glanced at the elf, then up at the sky where the fire dragons were swiftly drawing nearer. About to give up, he looked one last time at the map. His heart felt heavy, for he had truly hoped that this would work.

Something was changing! The arrow in the decorative compass was, miraculously, starting to spin. Faster and faster it turned, until it was nothing but a blur. The map's edges and creases, meanwhile, darkened subtly, gaining a rich golden hue. At the same time, tan-colored clouds began to swirl on the rest of the parchment. As the two of them watched eagerly, the clouds coalesced into recognizable shapes.

"It's Avalon—the root-realms!" exclaimed Tressimir. "Now . . . the map's coming closer, focusing on just one realm."

"Mudroot," declared the dragon. He glanced anxiously up at the sky. "But *where* in Mudroot?"

As if in answer, the map's image moved northward, past the plains of Isenwy, past the jungles of Africqua. At the farthest northern reaches of the realm, the map showed the dark, eerie outlines of a great swamp.

"The Haunted Marsh!"

As the dragon's voice echoed across the meadows, one of the centaurs shouted, "The time to fight has come! We face fire dragons by air, flamelons by land. Give us your command, Basilgarrad!"

Lifting his head, he roared, "All of you who can gallop— centaurs, horses, and deer—split into two groups and attack the flamelons from both sides. Elves, make good use of your bows! Then everyone on foot, you must charge the center to divide their lines. Show them your wrath—while the birds and I show ours to the fire dragons!"

A loud cheer erupted, combining the voices of many of Avalon's creatures. Despite Basilgarrad's grave concerns—the overwhelming numbers they must face, the dangers of fire in this realm, and that mysterious new weapon of the flamelons—he felt encouraged. For he knew that, while the invaders were motivated by greed and hatred, his forces were propelled by something much stronger. Their love for their homes and families—and for Avalon.

"Look!" cried Tressimir.

Basilgarrad, already starting to open his wings, turned to see the elf pointing at the map. The image of the Haunted Marsh was reforming, changing into a dark, shadowy scene. In its center stood a loathsome beast, writhing in a pit of corpses, drawing power from the death surrounding it. Though it had swollen in size, there could be no doubt: This was the same ghastly beast that Basilgarrad had seen before in the magical sphere. Blacker than night itself, it seemed to be not a body, but a void. Not a being, but a shadow. *Darker than dark*.

"That's it," growled the dragon. "That's who is behind all this."

"What is it?" asked Tressimir, grimacing at the sight.

"I don't know. But I will—"

The dragon halted, watching the image as it moved. What was so familiar about that shape? The writhing beast seemed to turn around, as if it were glaring directly at him. Suddenly there came a red flash, lasting only a split second before it faded into an angry, bloodred eye.

All at once, the truth struck Basilgarrad. "That leech—the servant of Rhita Gawr! Of course, that's it!"

Even as the memories of his encounters with the leech came flooding back to him, the map began to sizzle. Smoke curled up from the compass, then spread to the edges of the parchment. With a cry of surprise, Tressimir dropped the map—just as it burst into flames. Seconds later, nothing remained but ashes scattered on the ground.

Basilgarrad glowered at the ashes—and at the image of the swollen, shadowy leech in his mind. "I will find you," he growled. "Whatever happens, I will find you."

Raising his head, the dragon released a mighty roar. He leaped and rose skyward, plunging into battle for Avalon.

35: DOOMRAGA'S TRIUMPH

What you don't know can't hurt you. Until it does.

Deep in the darkness of the Haunted Marsh, Doomraga flashed its bloodred eye. Brighter than ever before, that signal pulsed through the air of Avalon, beyond the farthest reaches of the world, beyond the stars themselves—all the way to the spirit realm.

For that flash was a message to its master, the spirit warlord Rhita Gawr. A message that Doomraga had labored many years in this pit of death, swelling and contorting, to be ready to send. A message that meant the time had almost arrived for Rhita Gawr's conquest of Avalon.

Its body, darker than a shadow, suddenly shuddered. Within itself, enormous forces pushed to the surface. The shadow leech's skin bubbled and boiled. Then, with a bellowing cry, it opened its vast mouth.

Thousands and thousands of leeches, each one the length of a man's hand, poured out. Exploding into the air, these terrible minions floated upward, borne by Doomraga's magic. Rising on that evil wind, they flashed their bloodred eyes—announcing that they fully understood their mission.

To kill the green dragon, Avalon's last defense against Rhita Gawr.

Higher and higher they floated, rising out of the rotting fumes of the marsh. Then, clustering in a vile cloud, they flew eastward toward a great battle in Woodroot that had just begun. There they would descend on the dragon and his allies, killing them all.

Watching the minions depart, and knowing what was to come, Doomraga released a deep, raspy laugh. Even as its writhing body grew thinner again, its anticipation grew larger. Much larger. For it would soon bask in triumph as well as revenge.

Turn the page for a sneak peek at the next
installment of the Merlin saga:

BOOK 8

ULTIMATE MAGIC

PROLOGUE

For a big surprise, I look for a small mystery.

Basilgarrad lifted his enormous head, scanning the rolling meadows that reached to the distant trees. His dragon's eyes glittered as his powerful shoulder muscles tensed. Both of his furled wings—each one big enough to hold the entire body of a normal-sized dragon—shook with anticipation, their bony tips clattering against the scales of his back.

A breeze suddenly stirred, bending the blades of grass around him. To his own surprise, he caught some of his favorite scents. Dank woodland mushrooms. Cedar resins, both sharp and sweet. Tangy apples, so ready for eating they would almost peel themselves in a young elf's hands. Enchanted spiderwebs, sturdy enough to hold a boulder. Fresh spray from the headwaters of the River Relentless.

For an instant, taking in those rich aromas, he remembered why he treasured this realm, this world of so much life. So much magic. And why, if necessary, he would die to protect it.

His gargantuan tail, ending with a massive club, slammed against the ground. Tremors shot in all directions, cracking open crevasses in the meadows and shaking the faraway trees. For he had smelled, just then, a very different scent.

The scent of battle.

Allies, from all across Avalon, marched swiftly toward him. Muscular centaurs, stamping their hooves, loped to his side. Close behind came men and women who carried rakes and staffs and swords, elves who bore great hunting bows, and dwarves who shouldered double-bladed axes. Plus many other creatures ranging from burly bears to tiny field mice who brought nothing but their brave hearts.

More allies, too, dotted the sky. Eagles swooped down from the heights, hawks with bright red tails glided nearer, and owls floated out of the trees. Soon the air reverberated with their screeches, hoots, and cries.

Yet Basilgarrad peered past them all. For he was watching a dark swarm of jagged-winged warriors that had just appeared over the horizon. Fast they flew, coming closer by the second. He knew them all too well: fire dragons—over a hundred of them.

His nostrils flared. He could smell, even at such a distance, their charred scales and bloodstained claws. And he knew that only he had any hope of stopping them.

The great green dragon shifted his gaze—and what he saw made him dig his claws into the turf. Flamelon warriors! An immense mass of those battle-hardened warriors, trained beneath the smoky volcanoes of Fireroot, started to stream onto the meadow. Armor glinting, they marched steadily nearer. With them came powerful catapults, great machines that could fling heavy stones and vats of boiling oil. They also brought one more contraption, a pyramid-shaped tower so large that it took more than fifty flamelons to drag it across the ground.

Staring at the huge tower, whose wheels creaked noisily, Basilgarrad released a low, wrathful growl. *What in the name of Avalon is that thing?* he asked himself. *Whatever it is, I don't like it. Not at all.*

Although the mysterious tower made him feel uneasy, he quickly forgot about it, for his thoughts had turned to a far greater concern. The fate of his world, the Great Tree whose early days he had witnessed so long ago and whose many wonders he had seen over the centuries. Avalon was, as his friend Merlin once said, more than just a truly remarkable place. It was, in fact, an *idea*—that so many diverse creatures and realms could live together in peace, at least for a time.

That time, he knew, was now dead. But would Avalon itself die, as well? That depended on the outcome of this monumental clash. For this was going to be the first—and, most likely, the last—time all of Avalon's foes and defenders would face each other in battle.

As he scanned the approaching fire dragons and the fearsome battalion of flamelon warriors, he growled deep in his throat. He knew that if he and his loyal allies failed on this day, no one would be left to protect their world. Their homes, their dreams, their families and friends—even his beloved Marnya— would all be lost.

Forever.

His growl swelled into a rumble so loud that several centaurs reared up in surprise, their forelegs kicking at the air. *We must win this battle today!* His huge snout wrinkled. *Not just to defeat this enemy, and not just to save our loved ones. But for another reason, as well.*

"I must survive this day," he vowed, his voice rumbling like thunder. "To find and kill that evil monster behind all this!"

He thumped his tail, shaking with rage and frustration. He didn't know where to find that shadowy beast who had caused this war, promising priceless jewels to the dragons and unrivalled power to the flamelons. All he knew was that its secret lair was somewhere in Avalon—and that it served the wicked warlord of the spirit realm, Rhita Gawr. If only he knew where to look, he could destroy the beast and finally bring this horror to an end. And unless he did that, the threat to Avalon would only grow worse.

Grinding his rows of jagged teeth, he added in a somber tone, "The truth is, even if I do prevail today, there is no way to find that monster. No way at all."

"But there *is*."

Basilgarrad cocked his head and saw, peering up at him, Tressimir, the young historian of the wood elves. "What do you mean?" demanded the dragon. "Speak quickly!"

Tressimir reached into his weathered leather satchel and pulled out a folded piece of parchment. "This is a map. A magical map, from Krystallus. He wanted you to have it—to help you save Avalon."

Basilgarrad watched, glancing anxiously at the approaching enemies, as Tressimir unfolded the parchment. "This map can tell you where to find anything at all. Just concentrate on what you want to find. But first I must warn you."

"About what?"

"This map," declared the elf, "can be used only once. So whatever you want to find, you must be absolutely sure."

"I am sure!"

"Then concentrate your thoughts."

Filling his mind with the shadowy beast, as well as the terrors it had brought to Avalon, Basilgarrad stared at the parchment. Nothing happened. He thought harder, his whole enormous body trembling with exertion. Still nothing.

The parchment remained utterly blank.

Dismayed, he glanced at the swarm of fire dragons advancing across the sky. And at the army of flamelons, dragging their mysterious tower. Then, one last time, he looked at the parchment, silently cursing himself for being foolish enough to let it raise his hopes.

It was changing! The map's edges darkened to a rich golden hue, as tan-colored clouds started to swirl across its face. He spotted, in one corner, a decorative compass, whose arrow suddenly began to spin faster and faster. Meanwhile, the clouds coalesced into shapes. Recognizable shapes.

Avalon! All the root-realms appeared, then six out of seven vanished as the map focused on just one—Mudroot. Veering northward, the image moved all the way to the farthest reaches of the realm, revealing the dark, shifting outlines of a swamp. And deep within that swamp . . . an eerie red glow.

"The Haunted Marsh!" exclaimed Tressimir.

"So that's where you are hiding," growled the dragon through clenched teeth. "I will find you. Oh, yes, I will find you."

He rustled his gargantuan wings. "First, though, I have a battle to fight."

Just as Basilgarrad started to open his wings, Tressimir cried out in surprise. The map began to smoke, sizzling between his fingers. He dropped it, and at that instant, it burst into flames. Seconds later, nothing remained but ashes—and one tiny scrap that drifted slowly to the ground.

Deftly, Basilgarrad clasped the ragged bit of paper between the tips of two claws. The scrap, still smoking, looked more like a flake of charcoal than anything valuable. Let alone magical. Only a barely noticeable mark on its unburned edge, the golden arrow from the decorative compass, gave any hint of its remarkable origin.

On an impulse, he tucked the smoldering scrap into the gap above an iridescent green scale on his shoulder. Why, he couldn't explain. He only knew that he didn't want to part with it. At least not yet.

Then, opening his wide wings, he released a thunderous roar that filled the sky. All who heard it knew, beyond doubt, that the great battle for Avalon had begun.

1: THE ONSLAUGHT

Hope is sometimes fleeting, but always precious. Sad to say, when that battle began, most of my companions had no hope at all.

With a mighty roar that shook trees many leagues away, the most powerful dragon in the history of Avalon leaped into the sky.

But even as his enormous green wings opened wide and started to beat, slapping the air forcefully as they carried him higher, Basilgarrad glanced down at the spot where the ashes from the magical map were still drifting down to the grass. Silently, he repeated his vow: *I will find you. Whatever it takes, I will go to the Haunted Marsh—and find you.*

"But first," he said aloud, peering at the army of fire dragons flying swiftly toward him, "I have a small task to perform."

Eyes alight, he roared once again—the roar of a dragon plunging into battle.

Above him, a canyon eagle screeched, calling all the assembled hawks, owls, and eagles to their leader's side. As Basilgarrad rose higher to join them, his huge dragon wings shadowed the ground below—rolling grasslands that, in peaceful times, held only wildflower meadows and the bubbling springs that fed Woodroot's fabled River Relentless. For ages this place had been one of the most serene in Avalon. All that would soon change.

For now those meadows held a swollen tide of flamelon warriors, so seasoned that they marched in absolute unison, as if the metal of their armor and swords had been melted down and forged into a single weapon of death. From this altitude, he could see their many catapults, along with some smoking contraptions that he guessed were flamethrowers. And he could see, once again, the huge, pyramid-shaped tower whose ominous purpose could only be guessed.

Ogre's eyeballs! he cursed to himself. *What could that tower be?*

His gaze shifted from the flamelons and their machinery to his own scattered allies. Centaurs stamped their sturdy hooves, great bears roared angrily, elves readied their bows and arrows, while a few dozen brave men, women, and dwarves wielded spears and battle-axes. But seeing his supporters didn't fill him with hope. Rather, he shuddered at this aerial view. For it revealed just how vastly outnumbered his supporters were—and how they lacked the training, experience, and sophisticated weaponry of their foes. They looked less like an army, Avalon's last line of defense, than like a group of tattered moths about to be consumed by a blast of flames.

All they have, thought Basilgarrad grimly, *is their love for this world.* He flapped his wide wings, lifting his mountainous bulk so high that his massive tail stretched out fully behind him. *Well, I suppose they do have one more thing on their side.*

He suddenly curled his tail and snapped it, whiplike, against the air. The explosion smote the sky, louder than a hundred claps of thunder. Several of the approaching fire dragons faltered, veered out of formation, and probably would have turned tail and fled if their commanders hadn't roared angrily at them.

Allowing himself a smirk, Basilgarrad finished his thought. *They still have me.*

At that instant, twenty fire dragons at the attackers' leading edge simultaneously released a superheated blast of flames. Fire poured over Basilgarrad, so intense that he turned his face away to protect his eyes. Hot flames slammed into the protective scales of his neck and chest, blackening their once-radiant surfaces, but leaving him unharmed.

The brave birds flying at his side didn't fare so well. Two red-tailed hawks and one peregrine falcon with silver-tipped wings burst into flames, shrieked in agony, and plunged to their deaths. The canyon eagle's tail feathers caught on fire, though a swift tap from Basilgarrad's wing tip extinguished that. Meanwhile, far below, the shower of sparks fell onto the allied forces, causing screams from several whose hair, clothes, or skin had been burned.

Basilgarrad roared with rage—a powerful blast of air that blew backward several attackers' wings. Yet his roar, alas, carried no flames. As a woodland dragon, he couldn't breathe fire, no matter how hard he tried. No amount of volume could change that fact; as loud as his roar was, it seemed a weak response.

A raucous, rasping laughter echoed across the sky. "Is that all you can do?" taunted the fire dragons' leader. "That pitiable little snarl?"

He laughed again, a sound that scorched almost as badly as flames. A huge scarlet dragon, he was half again as large as his heftiest soldiers—though still smaller than Basilgarrad. His eyes blazed wrathfully, and his wings slapped the air with a vengeance. Upon his chin lay the stubbly remains of a once-prominent beard. It had been forcibly removed, long ago, by the only dragon who had ever dared to face him in battle: Basilgarrad himself.

"Well, well," answered the great green dragon, his own eyes glowing bright. He beat his wings slowly, hovering in place. "If it isn't Lo Valdearg, that orange snake with wings. I thought you wouldn't dare attack me again—at least until you grew another beard."

The fire dragon roared angrily, shooting a spray of sparks from his nostrils. "I do dare!" he bellowed, as sparks rained down on his snout.

"Only when you are flanked by a hundred soldiers," retorted Basilgarrad. His eyebrows, studded with iridescent scales, arched. "Because you wouldn't have the courage to attack me by yourself. No, without your army to help, you are afraid to fight."

"I would fight," boomed Lo Valdearg. "And I shall."

"Not likely! You are as cowardly as ever."

The fire dragon snorted with rage. "I am no coward!"

Basilgarrad's brows lifted higher. Would his foe really take the bait? Whatever his chances might be against this whole army—and they were slim at best—they would improve dramatically if he could tempt the leader to fight one-on-one.

Lo Valdearg spun in the air. "Wait here!" he commanded his soldiers. At once, the fire dragons ceased their advance. They hovered in the sky, flanking their leader as he flew alone into combat.

Unable to keep himself from grinning, Basilgarrad glided nearer, watching Lo Valdearg warily. At the same time, the fire dragon approached, raking the air viciously with his claws.

"Now we shall see who is truly the greatest dragon," rumbled Lo Valdearg as he started to circle his opponent.

"Yes, we shall." Basilgarrad, too, began to circle. "And we shall also see who is the greatest fool."

"That," snarled Lo Valdearg, "would be you." He grinned wickedly, showing hundreds of murderous teeth. "For only a complete fool would turn his back on his enemy!"

Too late, Basilgarrad realized the trap. While Lo Valdearg had always been ready to fight, he'd never intended to keep his word and fight alone. Instead, by circling, he had cleverly maneuvered Basilgarrad into position to be attacked from behind by an entire army of dragons.

The sky exploded with a terrible onslaught of flames— all directed at Basilgarrad. Amidst that deadly inferno of fire and smoke, he couldn't even be seen. The mighty roars of dragons, the sizzling crackle of flames, and the surprised screeches of hawks and eagles all filled the air. And with them came another sound—one dragon's raucous, rasping laughter.

The battle for Avalon had ended, it seemed, before it had even begun.